Down The Drain

Down The
Drain

John McColley

Contents

With thanks to Sadie, my first reader for life.

{ 1 }

Narayan Leon sat doubled over in the hospital chair, forehead pressed against his grandmother'sknobby right hand, wrapped in both of his own. In a frightening scene, replaying over and over in his mind, she had collapsed at dinner and lay unresponsive. The paramedics had scooped her up like a bundle of laundry and rushed her here, but the doctors were unable to rouse her. Machines beeped and hissed softly, some pumping life into her, others measuring their success. The air felt like it was split, separated into breathable and antiseptic components, which fought for the right to Nara's lungs. He worried vaguely about Gran's lungs, but it was the least of the worries crowding into the room around him, a biting insect buzzing in a room teeming with lions and serpents.

"Coma," he had overheard one of the doctors say, the melodramatic condition that the soap operas Gran loved threw around every other week. Her hand seemed so small, cold, and still, like she had slipped from the autumn of her years right into winter. The lions stretched, maws widening in massive yawns as he began to image life without her.

"You know I don't talk to you often, not without a curse waiting on my tongue," he addressed whatever deity was listening, his dark, wavy hair teasing his peripheral vision. He paced, striding on long runner's legs, arriving all too soon at a watercolor painting of flowers reflected in a pond. He saw his own thin face in the reflection of the glass; his eyes looked sunken, his high cheeks drawn.

He turned away, unable to look at himself anymore, hating that he believed, but in spite of the loss of his parents, his home, and his friends, he was also certain *something* was watching, *interfering*; "but this was a real low blow, man. You can't take her yet. If there's one person who deserved to be looked over for this whole 'mandatory dirt nap' thing, it's Gran, and you know it, even if you're *not* really omniscient. Not everything can be true, right? You can't be all knowing, all loving,

and all powerful, or this would be a very different world. But this?" Nara shook his head, feeling Gran's hand bones grind lightly under the pressure. He knew this wasn't the way to get what he wanted, even if there *was* someone listening, but he was angry. Gran had always been his one reason not to punch the whole world in the face. What would he do without her? What would he be?

Nothing. That was the only answer. He'd been working at the coffee shop to help Gran out in between classes, but could he do it just for himself? Take over the business? The building? That seemed far less... worth it and far scarier. Suffering hours of shilling donuts and coffee he could endure for her. She'd done it for him, his father and uncles. If it was going to be just him, though, why bother? Money? It seemed like such a stupid reason. Maybe for the people

Gran always called family, though most of them looked so different to his grandmother and him. Who were they really? These people who occupied Gran's building, the edges of his life.

"Hola, Nara," a soft voice said from the door.

He sat back in the beige chair in the beige room and nodded slowly, unable to say anything for the lump in his throat. He slid the chair back. It stuttered and shrieked against the floor. He winced and looked at Gran's passive face, then up at the visitor, Carmen, the coffee shop's baker, and the only person Nara knew who orbited Gran but didn't live in the building.

"Carmen... Good of you to come. I don't know what's going on... neither do the doctors. She just collapsed at dinner." The barrel of a man nodded, brown curls bobbing atop his head.

"Of course, of course, Nara. We're always here for both of you."

"'We?'"

"Eli, Saundra, Panx, and the others from... the coffee shop, and the building... The hospital folks wouldn't let us up, not 'family' on their little computer screens, but I slipped through." Nara could hardly visualize Carmen "slipping through" anywhere, especially unnoticed, but he nodded. However he did it, the man was here. "You want to watch the door for a minute?" Carmen waved him over while he strode to Gran's bedside.

Nara took position, moving through a cloud of the man's cologne, a tangy scent Nara associated with the baker. He stood just inside the door, though he wasn't sure what he was looking for. Carmen leaned over, whispering something to Gran.

"She can't hear you. Or, I dunno, maybe she can. I think I read that somewhere, but she can't answer, that's sure," Nara said. The lights in the hallway flickered, and the shadows in some of the unoccupied rooms' doorways deepened for a moment. He thought he saw a figure by the nurse's station, but when the lights stabilized again, there was no one.

Carmen had something in his hand now. It looked like a black and red strip of cloth, but when the man reached across with his other hand, Nara saw it was a long, tasseled pouch. Fingers pinched something from within and sprinkled it over the unmoving old woman.

"What are you doing now?" Nara asked, alarm in his voice, fear creeping up the back of his neck. With a flick of the baker's hand, the top flap of the pouch flipped forward and the whole thing vanished from sight. "Carmen!" He took a step forward.

"Excuse me, I'm sorry, but visiting hours are ending. You can come see your grandma tomorrow any time after 10am up to 8pm," a quiet, but unwavering, voice informed Nara from just behind him. He turned to respond, but the speaker had already moved on. He could vaguely hear her giving the same message to the next room. Though he couldn't make out the words, the cadence was the same, the roll and rhythm of the message like a song the woman had sung thousands of times.

"Gotta go, Carmen," Nara said, but the room was empty, quiet, beige as it had been minutes before. The only occupants were Gran and the machines monitoring her condition. "What the... Carmen?" There was no response, not that there was anywhere the broad baker could hide in the hospital room... The nurse had been blocking the door. He looked at the window, but it didn't look like it actually opened.

At a loss, Nara went back to Gran's side, taking up her other hand, careful to avoid disturbing the IV or wires. "I gotta go, Gran. You get some good sleep and wake up in the morning all fine, right? I'll see you then." Nara kissed the hand, cold, papery, and left the room.

He rode down the elevator with a young woman who stared at her feet, one hand clamped between those of a younger boy he imagined was her brother. Silence reigned behind the thin sonic veneer of cables and motors. He wanted to tell them they'd get through it, that it would get better, but remained silent. He certainly didn't feel like an authority on facing death, even though he had lived through enough of it. They parted ways at the entrance, lost in their own fogs, a loved one's death looming on the horizon, blotting all else out.

Nearly twenty people were waiting for him in the lobby, already standing, hands clasped before them, eyes cast down. When the elevator doors opened, a few looked up. Hands rose and spread like some kind of choreographed group hug in the making. He stopped short of walking into it.

"Thank you all for coming... I'm sure Gran would appreciate knowing you were here."

"We're all here for the Leons," Webster, a tall, thin, white man said, "Anything you need."

"Right now, I think I need to be alone. I know we're all going back to the same place, but if you could... give me a few minutes' lead, that would be great."

"Of course, Nara," said Mrs. Jatt, from beneath a helmet of gray hair that he could vaguely recall being black when he was little. A kind smile creased her face. He met a few sets of eyes on the way through the crowd, touching hands with many. Beyond the bright white and beige of the hospital, night had swathed the city in its own stiflingly hot, inescapable, embrace.

Nara turned left toward home, a memory of the sun, that had stored itself in bricks and concrete through the day, caressing his cheek. He held his hand up toward a wall. The energy was nearly tangible. Was this what ghosts were? Radiant lives absorbed by their surroundings? Released over time? Was this haunting? Would Gran haunt him? She had spent decades in that small apartment, the kitchen of the coffee shop. Surely every brick, every tile, every board was suffused with her vitality.

That thought lightened his step. What if she stayed? What if she could watch from the corner of the apartment kitchen, advising him on spices and rattling the hanging pots if he fell asleep on the couch, letting the water boil over? That would be something, more than he had of anyone else.

How did one sign up for being a ghost, anyway? He searched on his phone while he walked, swiping away from story after story of unfinished business and vengeance. Couldn't one remain from love? Just because seeing family here was better than whatever came after? By the time he arrived at his home over Leon's Coffee Shoppe, he was deep into reading about how to capture souls and keep loved ones from slipping away.

Dinner lay half eaten, hours cold. He passed through the kitchen without even the thought of cleaning up. The whole apartment was damp with the steam from cooking and redolent with saffron and pimentón. Gran had never been a loud woman, but in health, Aizah Leon was like a songbird, flitting from branch to branch, visiting neighbors, knitting, cooking, hands always performing some act of creation or comfort. The stillness in the apartment felt unnatural.

Nara opened a couple of windows, hoping for a cross breeze, but there was no more movement in the air at three stories than at street level. The night sounds of the city greeted him again after minutes of the solitude of his own breath, his own footsteps in the stairs and hallway. He welcomed the proof of not being alone, without the actual presence of others. The silence had been too heavy, too soon.

He stood, listening to traffic and indecipherable conversation through the window, his brain wrapped in wool, until a low knock at the door. The room seemed a few shades less dark, even in contrast to the wash of neon signs. The clock above the TV told him it was nearly eleven, via an unnatural blue glow that flickered yellow and then red. He'd left the hospital hours ago... The knock came again, same pattern, but more insistent.

"Coming," he croaked, his throat dry. He swallowed and repeated himself, trying to remember how to get his feet to move across the room. He felt dizzy but stuck in syrup. Eventually, he dragged one foot in front of the other. Opening the door, he found no one, but an envelope had been stuck in the letterbox Gran had hung on it to receive checks and notes from her tenants. The two floors above the coffee shop contained a total of eight apartments, including her own. Friends of the family occupied the rest. Everyone Nara knew, it seemed, aside from people at school and Carmen, lived within the brownstone.

The envelope bulged. Someone's late night rent delivery. Gran charged decades out of date rates, barely enough to pay the taxes and keep the lights on in the coffee shop. "But what else do we need? And why should we take it from them? They're family," she would always say when one of his uncles suggested she raise rates.

His uncles... all gone "across the water" as Gran called it, not in some ominous way most people referred to death, but as though she might hop on a boat for a visit any time.

There was no movement in the hallway, no hint of the visitor. Nara took the envelope and closed the door quietly. Whoever it was, no doubt put their name or apartment number in the envelope. He dropped it on the table, as he passed, and then lay on his bed, flopping down atop the covers.

2

Nara noticed two things as his consciousness settled into dreaming: one, that it was raining, something he could not recall ever witnessing in a dream; and two, that he could hear whispers all around him, a demanding susurrus of sibilant voices. Each drew his attention, accompanied by a flash of a face, or a place, and emotion. A constant stream of ups and downs and sideways made way for the next and the next and the next before he could process them. He spotted a tree and made for its shelter, huddling between the roots as the moisture rolled off him. He took stock of his position. Sand sloped down toward a sea, but not like any sea he had seen.

Amid the waves of too-blue water floated all manner of unimaginable things. No, that was exactly it. That's *just* what they were, imaginable, purely imaginable. A castle of pink crystal bobbed by, pulled by a team of narwhals. A mound of papers drifted in the current, spinning slowly and in roughly the opposite direction to the castle. A school of lion fish that were actually half lion and half fish... *Merlions?* he wondered, cavorted in the waves until they caught the scent of something and sped off toward a colorful windmill sitting on the back of a great turtle. A small forest sprung up around the windmill's base, each plant a variation on the Christmas tree. Myriad other sights he didn't have time to process threatened his grip on reality.

"Reality," said a slow, rye voice, "who needs it?" Before Nara could answer, a rainbow-colored serpent, as wide as his outstretched arms, slithered into view. The creature addressed him again, voice like pouring honey, "Oh, you're from... 'Up there,' how lovely. Not much makes it down here... in one piece. How did you do it? Do you... have a way back? An anchor?"

"Back? Anchor?" Nara asked.

"Mmm, we *are* new, aren't we? Accident or sickness? I suppose it doesn't matter much now, though either could lead to yo-yoing..." As the snake spoke, Nara felt himself lift from the sand. He grabbed at the branches of the tree as he rose, but they were all out of reach. "Ah well, see you later, then. What was your name?"

"Na-!" He began to respond, then succumbed to a barrage of raindrops and their associated memories.

***

Nara jerked awake. The day was in full swing based on the traffic sounds and light pressing through the curtains. Rain pattered against the window.

Slowly, he trudged through the chores of scraping the dinner plates and depositing them in the dishwasher before preparing himself breakfast. He made too many eggs and an extra slice of toast before his cloudy mind connected his emotional stupor with the reality that Gran was in the hospital. He forced himself to eat, then went to her bedroom to gather some of her things: a favorite sweater, the book she was reading that he could read to her to draw her back to him, and whatever else seemed appropriate.

On opening the first cabinet, he was struck by the idea that he didn't really know his Gran at all. Here were not balls of yarn and large, blunt needles, or cardigans she'd knitted, but a collection of candles with wax dripped over brass holders, pictures of his parents and uncles and grandfather in lace frames, incense sticks, brass bowls, scarlet doilies and things that looked too much like bundles of small animal bones; all bound with strips of leather and red string, hanging from the upper edge of the enclosure, for him to want to investigate further.

"Gran, what are you into?" Unable to deal with the voodoo altar, or whatever was going on in the cabinet, Nara closed it and backed away, moving to the closet he was fairly sure had sweaters in it. Still, he hesitated at the door and opened it with his shoulder against the edge, ready to slam it shut if real skeletons or demons lunged at him. Seeing only a familiar rainbow of sweaters and dresses, most of which Gran had knitted or sewn herself, and a neat rack of shoes, Nara heaved a sigh and picked a few sweaters and a canvas tote bag to carry everything before quickly closing the door. He didn't dare try her drawers but surveyed her bed for a small blanket or throw pillow before recalling that stuff would still be on the couch.

Packed, Nara was leaving through the kitchen when he spotted the envelope. He'd have to figure out where to deposit the money; though if Gran didn't wake up, money in the bank would be locked up until her will was read... did she have a will? He wasn't sure, but he resolved to raise the difficult subject if the woman did wake, to prepare them both for the inevitable.

Optimistically, he stuffed the envelope into the bag in case Gran was in a state to tell him her account number, or at least where her banking paperwork was. That led him to thinking about opening more doors and drawers in her room. Nope. He wouldn't be poking around unless he had to.

Halfway down to the coffee shop, his phone buzzed in his pocket.

"Oh, hey Eli, what's up?"

"'What's up?' What's 'up' is that it's seven am and we've got a line down the block, but no Carmen. No Carmen means-"

"No donuts. Man... I'm headed down now. Be there in five seconds. You called him?"

"Yeah, I called him. No answer. Almost called your grandmother, too, but-"

"Yeah, and now it's on me," Nara said as he trotted down the last flight of stairs and shoved open the door into the shared hallway with an elbow.

"Sorry, little man," Eli said through the phone, but then they were eye to chin. The older Black man's face showed more concern than any further words could have conveyed. "What's the plan?" he said finally.

"If you can hold down the fort with the coffee, I'll stop by Carmen's on the way to the hospital. Gran wasn't... she was in a coma when they kicked me out last night. I'm bringing her some things in case she wakes up. I was going to spend my day before my shift there, but if things are crazy, I'll come right back."

"I've got this. You just nudge Carmen, maybe dump a bucket of cold water on him, and send him down. I know it's late to start, but we'll lose hundreds if we go without donuts for the whole day, not to mention the rep hit. People who can't rely on their regular order might go somewhere else." Nara nodded.

"I get that. You're absolutely right. I'll roust Carmen and be back for damage control as soon as I can."

"Thanks. You're a good grandson. You'll make a good boss when your turn comes."

"Thanks, Eli. I just hope it's later than sooner."

"I hear ya. Good luck," Eli said, hand warm on Nara's back for a moment before the older

man turned away to face the tide of unhappy customers.

3

Narayan had thought the crowd on the sidewalk outside the coffee shop had been a tangle of metropolitan chaos. What he found at the corner of Chamberlain St and 10th was a full on circus. At the foot of the nearly two century old, six story brownstone, with arches over the main entrance and some rows of windows, fire trucks, ambulances, police cars, all with lights flashing, clogged Chamberlain in both directions. The entire intersection was cordoned off. A sea of people, from gawkers to the media, ebbed and flowed against the yellow tape shoreline, stoic officers like lighthouses keeping anyone from crashing onto the rocks.

"Matty Stephens here with Action Eye News, channel 113," a middle-aged woman announced into a camera, her back to Carmen's building. "Authorities aren't revealing what happened here at the 200 block of Chamberlain St early this morning, but as you can see, every window in the building appears to have been painted black from the inside. No one has had any communication with the residents since before midnight last night, and no one has come out, or gone in, since. It's quite a mystery. Is it some kind of terrorist attack? A plumbing mishap? A quick growing black mold? Who can tell? Updates as things develop here. Back to you Rob." The woman's mic-hand dropped, and hung by her side, as she turned to stare up at the six floors of apartments. "What the hell do you think is going on in there, Rodolpho?" she asked the cameraman. He only shrugged broad shoulders, fiddling with something on the camera. He was even bigger than Carmen.

Nara hadn't noticed as he'd approached, distracted by all the activity below, but what Matty had said was true: every single window was a yawning void of darkness. What was going on? Carmen disappearing from the hospital, then... disappearing, flickering figures... Gran...

While the front of the building was mobbed, the workers securing the side and rear entrances were encumbered by yellow-taped saw horses. Nara knew he had to get in there, to check on the chubby baker who told tall tales of playing baseball in Cuba in his youth, the game being his ticket to the US. He moved almost without thinking, outpacing the officers and firefighters moving the barriers and turning the corner only to find the back entrance guarded by another patrol car.

Not wanting to seem suspicious, Nara kept walking across the street to the row of brownstones. He went right up the stairs.

"Hey! I know you!" One of the officers called at his back. He climbed another step. "Yeah, Nara, right? You got some donuts?" Caught, identified before he had a chance to learn thing one. He turned, plastering on his best customer service smile.

"Sorry, officer, the donut guy didn't show up this morning. It's actually a pretty big problem."

"No donuts? You want me to put out an APB?" the officer half-joked.

"Nah, I think I know where he is. Just getting to him is proving a challenge..." Nara involuntarily looked up at the blacked-out building, then realized what he'd done and more obviously turned and looked over his shoulder at the building he was going into.

"Ah, yeah, a real mess over here. Don't let me keep you, then," the officer said, waving him on. Nara passed through the small foyer easily, as the inner door's lock had been broken for ages, and went down the first floor hall to a door marked "Maintenance". This one had a trick to it that Nara knew from his time dating a girl who lived on the third floor. He lifted the whole door, pulling up the handle, then twisted. Freeing the door, he pulled it open and stepped through into the dark.

This darkness wasn't mysterious, though. It was ordinary, accompanied by the mustiness of a damp basement. He shook his phone to activate the flashlight and jogged down the concrete steps to a room lined with electrical boxes on the left and storage shelves on the right, piled with dusty boxes. A gray metal door, behind a set of shelves at the opposite end, easily slid open with a small screech.

A gasp came from somewhere back up the stairs. Turning, Nara spotted a wash of light on the bare wall of the landing. He suppressed the urge to demand who was there, given he wasn't supposed to be there either. Instead, he doused his own light and slipped through the crack between door and frame to hide in the shadows.

"Which way did he go?" a woman's voice asked.

"Looks like there's only one way," a man's voice answered. The light panned across the open door, blinding Nara before he could look away. He tried to flatten himself against the wall, but the narrow tunnel didn't leave much room for him to hide.

"We can see you," the woman said flatly. "Just come out. We're not going to bust you."

"What do you want? Why are you here?"

"We could ask you the same."

"Aim your light away." The camera rig and its lights drifted off to the side.

"Is this a way into the building across the street? The blackout building?" the woman asked.

"Yes, my friend lives over there. He didn't show up to work this morning. I need to know what happened to him. Everyone's worried."

"And where is this? This workplace?"

"Leon's Coffee Shoppe. He's the baker, makes donuts, other pastries, bread for sandwiches," Nara said.

"We're sorry for your friend but getting the scoop on whatever's going on over there, that's worth big points with my bosses. I could get a promotion, sit behind the big desk instead of getting rained on and... Never mind that. Can you get us through? I'll pay you. Two hundred."

"Dollars?"

"Three? I don't think I have any more on me. Come on kid, we won't cause you any trouble. Just get us in. We can find our way back out."

"Uh... I guess, sure..." Nara said, knowing that it felt like a bad idea, just as bad as going in there at all, but he was going anyway. May as well pick up a few bills.

He shoved open the door, and the woman held out a thin stack of fifties. "Uh, thanks." Nara stuffed the money into his pocket. "It's just straight through, really, but there are a couple of spots where the floor's bad. Pretty sure the tunnel's like a hundred year old, Prohibition, or whatever."

"That makes sense... A lot of those places had secret entrances and passwords and such," the woman said. "I'm Matty-"

"Stephens, yeah, I caught your act on the street. He's Rodolpho. I'm Nara. Let's go." He turned away from the light and picked his way past a small collapse, where the wall had succumbed to time, and then they were off for almost fifty feet before the first weak spot. "Stay left, then at the brick, stay right. There's a bit of a jump up here, where the whole width of the floor is busted out, but you can see it easy enough." He demonstrated these directions, putting his hands out to the walls to support himself as he jumped over the gap. He skidded to a stop and turned to look down. Was that water gurgling below? He supposed it didn't matter. Anyone falling down there probably wasn't coming back.

"Seriously? I have to jump? With the camera?" Rodolpho said.

"Unless you've got rockets in that pack," Nara replied.

"Aren't there any loose boards, or a door or something down there, you can bring back to make a bridge?"

"Man, I don't have time for this. I have to check on my friend and then get to the hospital for my Gran. This day is already about eighty-nine degrees off normal."

"Ok, well Matty, you can go, but I can't risk that jump."

"There's no point in going if you're not there to document," Matty said. "I'll talk to the channel about a raise for you."

"Pssh yeah..."

"Really this time. This is our big break! No one else is getting this footage!" she insisted. "They can't deny us!" Empowered by her own speech, she backed up a few steps from the edge and took a running leap. Nara caught one elbow, to help her keep her balance, but she landed safely. Luckily, reporting didn't require showing her feet, so she wore sneakers.

"You're seriously going to get me killed one of these days," Rodolpho sighed. "Be ready to catch me, yeah?"

"Of course," Matty promised, though Nara knew it would be his responsibility to risk himself if the larger man didn't make it under his own power. He thought about looking for that board the cameraman had mentioned, or a rope, or even a sheet to twist into a rope, but then the man backed up a few steps and ran toward him. He prayed quietly instead.

Rodolpho took a final step to launch himself. The stone beneath his feet crumbled with the sudden weight. He cried out and pitched forward, slamming into the stone on the far side. Nara crouched and grasped one beefy arm, then hauled back with his own legs. Rodolpho squirmed and kicked. More rocks fell into water somewhere below, but finally, Matty grabbed the man's other arm and they managed to get him up. Camera, man, and floor somewhat worse for wear, the trio continued down the tunnel.

"I hope you know another way out. I don't think we're going back that way," Matty said.

"I'm sure as hell not," agreed Rodolpho. "I lost three buttons from my shirt, a knob off the camera, and my belly's all scraped up."

"All in the name of greatness, Rodolpho, come on. Let's get in there and get our scoop," Matty urged.

{ 4 }

The other end of the tunnel was hidden in an old store-room which was still used to harbor moldering boxes and dusty bottles. Nara wasn't certain what to expect, when they opened the secret door, but it certainly wasn't what he saw.

The past was on display in threads and clouds of vaguely luminous shadow, humanoid forms brightened further by ethereal golden lanterns and a stream of glowing blue music weaving its way from the Stygian instruments of a jazz quartet on a small stage at one end of the room. Flappers flapped and jitterbugs jittered on the dance floor, while others whispered to one another and clinked glasses at small, round tables and along a dusty bar backed by hundreds of unmarked bottles and a long, foggy, mirror. Nara batted at the streamers of darkness; they clung to his hand for a moment, trailing behind like streamers. Eyes wide, he shook the clinging shadows off and watched them bend and reform into layers like oil settling on water. What was going on? A shadow bartender nodded at them.

"Take a seat anywhere. One of the girls will take your order promptly." The whisper was nonetheless perfectly clear through the din, as though the words had been funneled directly into Nara's brain. He stood still, processing the scene before him. How was any of this possible? Were these things just visions? Or was there danger here?

"Which way? I can't see anything in this dark," Matty said.

"Yeah, the lights on the camera aren't cutting through this... whatever it is. It's not smoke. I can breathe just fine," Rodolpho said.

"Dark? I mean, sure, there's a darkness to it, but all the lamps. The music itself weaving through the air like... magic... Dios mío!" Nara's already racing heart throttled up.

"What is- Aaaaaah!" Matty screamed. Rodolpho screamed.

Five shadow-wreathed forms, more solid than the rest, sat at two pushed-together tables to their left. Nara advanced, peering at the bodies. They weren't exactly skeletons, but their skin was gray, pulled taut, showing every tooth, their eyes sunken, hidden in shadow, or missing, Nara couldn't tell. He shivered.

Their clothes seemed somehow familiar. Then an earring glinted in the camera's lights. It was a distinctive gold hummingbird with a tiny diamond chip eye. Nara's heart leapt into his throat. This had all been kind of a spectacle to this point, but here was...

"Paulina?" Nara whispered in disbelief, bending over the table for a closer look at the earring. There was no mistake. He fought back tears. What would she be doing down here? Placing one resident of his building, he quickly recognized a watch on another wrist and a tattoo on the back of a desiccated hand, running up the impossibly thin forearm he remembered as being quite robust. No... NO! He lost his battle with the fluid leaking from his eyes.

"You know her?" Matty asked. Nara nodded.

"I know all of them. Friends... family. They lived in the apartments over the coffee shop. I saw most of them every day."

"Hmm, another tie between the coffee shop and this building... curious. What do you think it means? None of them were mad scientists, were they? Experimenting down here?" Matty asked.

"Does this place look like a laboratory?" Nara snapped, a tide of emotion threatening to overwhelm him. How would he tell Gran? "No... No, I'm sorry. It's just that... I *knew* them. They were good people. Paulina helped me with my math homework. Gustavo always had me run to the corner store for him, but he'd give me money to buy candy for myself, too... These people were my family."

"I'm sorry... What were they doing down here?" Matty asked. Rodolpho zoomed in on each face in turn. Nara wanted to bat the camera from his hands at the disrespect but held back. They *should* be remembered. If they were all victims of... whatever this was, they might even provide evidence of what had happened.

"Maybe they were visiting with Carmen when whatever happened... happened. I can see some of them enjoying the idea of drinking in a speakeasy, even if the decorations and doorman were a century gone," Nara said. "But why is it like *this*? All these lamps and music... Maybe they could see it, too..."

"I don't hear any music. See? What do you see? Are you alright? Did you hit your head in the passage back there? Maybe you should just stay here, and we'll go on ahead, investigate, shoot some on site footage," Matty said. Rodolpho looked at her. "What? He'll be fine, unless he's allergic to dust."

"You're only trying to convince yourself, Matty," Rodolpho said. "Look man, you can head back. Young guy like you can probably make that jump again. I don't know how safe it really is in here, with all this fog stuff. We'll be sure to tell emergency services about your friends when we see them."

"No, I need to find Carmen. He's not down here with the others. I've been looking, and I'm sure. He has a gold tooth. None of these... people... do. He must be upstairs somewhere. Maybe he went up to get more drinks for the party or something."

"Yeah. Maybe. Hold onto that, man. That's the way out, right? Where you were headed before we found your friends?" Rodolpho asked gently. Nara nodded slowly.

"The entrance is right there, guarded by the big guy. Between the lights."

"Big guy?" Rodolpho asked, apprehension growing in his voice.

"Lights?" Matty asked in turn.

"Yeah, it's a hoppin' scene or however they used to say it. There's dozens of people, or something like them... ghosts, maybe? Memories? Something... Something I think my Gran told me about when I was little."

"Hey, hun, what can I get ya?" A spectral waitress wearing a short skirt and short sleeved blouse, both jet black, flesh limned in a pale yellow, asked. She carried a tray of empty glasses.

"Nothing, thanks, just passing through," Nara said with a forced smile. He dodged dancers and other waitresses, eyeing the bouncer and trying to determine if the other would keep him from leaving through his post.

"What was that? Who were you talking to? Why are you moving like that?" Matty asked, eyes narrowing.

"The dancers and servers," Nara responded, focused on the man by the door.

"The who and what?" Matty asked, voice tighter. "Do you know what he's talking about? It's just dark. Like stringy, creepy dark, but there's no people or anything, aside from your... Are you feeling ok?" Matty looked back and forth between Nara and Rodolpho as she spoke.

"I've been messing with settings, and I'm picking up some kind of interference, vaguely people-shaped... You don't think this place is... haunted?" Rodolpho asked, tension in his voice increasing.

"Every window in the place went black and we went through half the phone numbers Jimmy gave us for people who live here. We got no response, not a single one, text or voice. I think 'haunted' is as reasonable an assumption as any," Matty said, trailing after Nara as he wove his way across the space and stood before a door.

"Mind if we just head through? My friends and I... need some fresh air."

"This is what youse could call an 'emehgency exit,'" the shade said, crossing massive arms before his equally voluminous chest. "Take the tunnel if youse need out."

"The tunnel is, um... There's a hole opened up in the floor. It's not safe."

"Safa than you tryin' to get through this doah and distuhbin' the disguise on the otha side," the bouncer countered.

"Please, it's important. I swear we won't get you busted. We just need to get into this building unseen. We'll uh, set things back up when we get through, make it look perfect," Nara said.

"What are you doing? Just go through the door," Matty insisted, nudging Nara forward. As he stumbled a partial step toward the bouncer, the man's arms unfolded and hands came up to either side of his chin. A fist as big as Nara's face rocketed toward him. Nara dodged to the side, turning away, but felt a cold shock behind his ear. White stars exploded in his vision. He staggered, catching himself against the back of a booth. Doubling over, he threw up what little breakfast he'd managed to eat onto dusty, cracked, hundred-year old leather.

"What is happening?" Matty demanded, somewhat more hysterical.

"Let me fiddle with my filters some more," Rodolpho said, reaching into a fanny pack with shaky hands. Nara pushed himself back upright.

"I don't want to fight," he said, rubbing the back of his head, "I just need to check on Carmen. He lives upstairs. The cops are outside."

"The cops are outside right now? Youse could have said somethin'!" the bouncer replied. He reached up to a cloth rope dangling near the door and hauled on it, setting off a series of bells along the top of the wall. A dozen deluges of dust drifted down from decades-dormant devices.

"Holy shit, what's that?" Matty demanded, grabbing the back of Nara's arm with manicured talons. As soon as the bells began, the band stopped playing, and the dancers ran for the secret passage and rushed toward the door where the bouncer was. Icy blasts shot through Nara over and over as the door was thrown open and Prohibition spirits fled. Dizzy, supporting himself with a hand on the wall, he staggered toward the now open door. "How did you do that?"

"I didn't. Those ghosts were just really afraid of the cops, I guess. Let's go," Nara said shakily, but resolved, now that the door was open.

{ 5 }

Carmen lived on the fifth floor, not exactly a penthouse, especially not in this part of town, but it had afforded a fine view of the city before a steel and glass forest had grown up from the East Side, cutting off lines of sight to the bay.

Apartment doors stood open, almost every one. Nara called into these voids, and knocked on the closed doors they passed on the first floor, on the way to the stairs at the opposite end of the building.

"Are you sure you should be doing that? What if they're like... *zombies* or something?" Rodolpho asked.

"Hush, don't be absurd, just start rolling," Matty demanded. She reeled off her name and channel and how amazing it was that she was getting the one and only exclusive peek into the great mystery of the day. She had Rodolpho pan across a handful of doorways, hoping, no doubt, for more shots of corpses in agonized positions, or dramatically ruined homes strewn with glass and ceramic from people collapsing during a meal, or maybe a lone surviving pet crawling out of the shadows on hearing human voices.

None of those things made themselves evident. It was as if everyone had just walked out of their apartments into oblivion.

On the second floor, Nara heard moaning coming from one of the apartments. He held up a hand for the others to wait, then set the tote down by the door. Peering into the darkness, he saw a form lying on a couch. He stepped past the threshold, seeing pictures of a family hanging at odd angles on the wall, surrounded by ghostly edges of peeling and curling wallpaper. The faded columns of flowers seemed to sway and shift as he crept forward.

"Hello? Are you alright?" Nara called in a low tone.

"Help me, please..." a man groaned.

"What's wrong? How can I help you?"

"Water... I need water..." Nara stepped farther inside, slowly, gingerly, as though the floor might fall out from under him at any second. He saw the man, sores all over his face, his arms bare. He was thin, the underlying skeleton lending more to the topography of his form than muscle or fat did.

In the kitchen, Nara found a glass in a rack by the sink and ran the tap. He did it automatically but then realized it was probably odd that the plumbing still worked when the lights didn't. He wondered if the water was okay to drink.

Trying to work this out, as he returned to the small main room of the apartment, he knelt beside the figure and held out the water. The man's hand passed through the glass like a gentle wave rolling up to shore. When his fingers grazed Nara's though, the youth was thrown back by a blast of cold energy, slamming into the wall. He saw stars, white against the black room. He retched but had already emptied his stomach back in the speakeasy.

After a few moments, the apartment stopped spinning around him and he spotted the glass. It was lying over, its contents darkening the worn carpet, but the man was gone.

"All right in there?" Matty called.

As he pulled himself together, Nara thought about the blow the bouncer had struck him. This more recent hit was far stronger despite the spirit's emaciated form and incidental touch. Whatever was powering these apparitions was growing as they rose through the building. A few more floors, and he might not survive such a collision. Nara crawled back into the hallway. As he did, the voices became louder, clearer to him. They were all around.

"I don't think we should make any more detours," he said breathlessly.

"What happened? Trip over something?" Rodolpho offered him a hand up. Taking it, Nara let the other man pull him to his feet.

"Not exactly, it looks like someone might have died, moaning for help, stuck on the couch. Sounds like he's not the only one. They must have had something tear through here like wildfire. Spanish flu, maybe? Or something we don't even think about today because scientists cured it? It sounds like Hell's own symphony of suffering." It seemed as if interacting with the first had woken the rest or maybe opened his own ears to hear. What could be up there, that it would activate whatever small residues of the former tenants of this place clung to its sinew and bone?

"Wow, you hear all that? Like a medium? Can you ask them questions? Maybe one of them knows what's happening here," Matty suggested.

"Not a bad idea," Rodolpho agreed. "I've been getting static that might have EVPs, but I can't really tell. Whenever they play those on ghost hunting shows, I can never hear what they claim the ghosts are saying."

"That's because ghost hunting shows are ridiculous trash TV. At best, they're perpetuating myths and making a buck off advertisers. At worst, they're giving people false hope about contacting loved ones and opening them up to swindlers," Nara said with disgust. Gran had spoken out against these kinds of shows, whether on TV or the street, since he could remember. He guessed it had rubbed off on him.

"Don't hold back now. Tell us how you really feel," Rodolpho said.

"The channel has two hit ghost hunting shows, and Tyler Tyler Talks, so don't say any crap like that while we're rolling," Matty said. Ugh, Tyler Tyler. A charlatan if ever there was one. Nara wondered what kind of people he'd led in here. Then he remembered the three hundred dollars and wondered if he was one of them now. The thought turned his stomach, which had barely recovered being worked over by the plague ghost.

"If you see any black forms, and I'm guessing you might as we get closer to the source of the problem and they get more energized, don't touch them. Don't let them touch you."

"Suddenly you're an expert?" Matty pressed.

"After just taking a bunch of hits from them? The most recent unintentional but much more powerful? Yes, I'd say I have enough experience to advise you *not to touch the ghosts*," Nara snapped. "Can we go, please? We've got a ways to climb." Far above, something howled. Oh goody. Nara heaved another sigh and walked on.

{ **6** }

Now as they climbed the stairs, it was all the trio could do to avoid more anachronous scenes like the speakeasy. They passed another story of spirits rolling around and moaning on the floor, seen through open apartment doors, the landings and common areas, even the hallways. Matty remained blissfully unaware, but Rodolpho eventually found a filter and setting that made him gasp.

"You're not going to believe this, Matty," he said. "Some of them are more in focus than others, like they fade with time maybe? Laying everywhere, crawling, tussling with each other. The kid wasn't joking when he talked about Hell earlier. How many people have died here over the last couple of centuries? How many are stuck in their final moments?"

Voice trembling as she reined in her apprehension, Matty said, "You're right, I wouldn't believe it. Not even going to look. Don't need to distract myself with any... smudges you will mass-hysteria me into thinking are hundred year old hookers and factory workers." It was clear to Nara that his own consistent reactions to the dark visions all around him were at least partly convincing her, and she didn't want to be convinced. He supposed he didn't blame her.

"I wonder why we haven't seen any residents, like current, living ones, or at least... ones that were living yesterday..." Rodolpho said as they crept along. He was filming, getting shots of everyday scenes interspersed with historical nightmares. Disease, violence, and fire were common neighbors in the rougher part of town. Nara flinched at more than one ghostly gunshot that Matty seemed not to hear.

"So what's your angle?" Nara asked. "What are you hoping to report?"

"I suppose we'll have to figure that out after the fact. I can't see what's going on, and there don't seem to be any clues as to the source of the darkness."

"Don't worry, I'm getting it all. This would make an amazing found-footage horror film," Rodolpho said. "I just hope nobody else finds it on *our* corpses..."

"Helpful," Matty said sarcastically. "Does it seem to either of you to be emanating from anywhere? Like is it thicker in one area? Or flowing in a direction so we can follow it back to its source?" Nara thought about the question before answering, looking around at the swirling thinner strands, sheets of black, and pillars like humans bound up in spiderwebs of shadow.

"It's all kind of just spinning around I think. Maybe toward the middle of the building and up of course. I still need to find Carmen, if I can."

"But we haven't seen anyone, like *anyone*," Matty reminded him. "Where could they have all gone?"

"Did you hear that?" Rodolpho asked in a ragged whisper. Nara had thought he'd heard something, something distant. A thump. It came again, this time from above and the other end of the hallway.

"What is it?" Nara wondered, directing his attention upward as though he would be able to divine the answer.

"Ghosts knocking stuff over? Look at all the doors that have been left open. Maybe something made people look out in the hallway, a commotion?"

"Lady, we're deep in the West Side. Everyone knows better than to look out the window, let alone open their door when they hear noises. 'Nothing but trouble lay that way,' as my Gran says."

"Then how did all these doors get opened? Did something mind control them into opening up? One by one or en masse? Is this some kind of zombie flick?" Matty asked, staring into the camera.

Nara heard another thump, much closer, and grabbed the other two by the arms, backing into an open doorway and dragging them with him as the stairwell door at the end of the hall exploded outward. Deeper darkness poured down the hall like roiling storm clouds, surging across the doorway, obliterating the ribbons and streams of deepest darkness with a solid, impenetrable, wall of black. Even the camera's lighting rig did nothing to discern even the merest eddy or streak.

"Holy crap! Don't do that!" Matty cried out, batting at the sleeve of her blazer to smooth it out. Then she saw the pitch black doorway and changed her tune. "Oh, wow... Uh, thanks. Thanks for saving us. Sorry about the yelling."

"I don't know if we're saved yet," Nara said, leaning against the wall as the other two stepped into the small apartment's living room. A TV stood against the wall shared by the hall, a rough, pilly corduroy couch across the middle, and a small table with two chairs between the two windows, which, like all the others, were completely blacked out.

"It's not coming in... Why isn't it coming in?" Matty asked.

"Maybe it works like vampires," Rodolpho replied, "Nobody invite it in."

"Not much chance of that," Matty agreed.

Nara looked around. Like most of the other apartments they'd peeked into on the way up to Carmen's floor, there was no one home. A thinner miasma of shadow hung layered in the air, but the outer walls were blanketed, blocking all daylight and even sounds from outside. He couldn't hear a single siren or motor. In fact, the place was stone quiet, except for their breathing and footsteps.

"Help!" A voice, younger, female, called from the deeper dark of the doorway. "Matty!"

"Lois?" Matty asked, taking a half step toward the door. Nara hooked her arm.

"It's not her. It's just a clumsy trick. Horror movie classic 'pretend to be a loved one to lure the characters out of their refuge,' stuff," he told her.

"It's... my little sister..." Matty said, voice shaking. "She... She died over twenty years ago, when we..." She pulled her arm from Nara, trying to get to the rectangle of black.

"It's not your fault, Matty. I don't blame you..." The voice said sweetly. Nara stepped past Matty and slammed the door, standing between it and her, hands up, ready to catch her if she reached for the handle.

"Don't listen to it. That's not your sister. Whatever that is might not even have a face, or a body at all. It's doing whatever it did to everyone else here last night," Nara said. "It's like sirens, the mythological kind, luring sailors onto rocks. Don't be a foolhardy sailor." He wondered if he would be so strong, so logical, if it was his mother's voice, or Gran's...

"What do we do now?" Rodolpho asked. "If it wants us to go out there, then we don't want to go out there, so where *do* we go? *Can* we go anywhere? How long will this last? Do we have food? Water? Air? Is this black stuff poisonous?" Nara stared at Rodolpho, head hanging to one side.

"Can we keep it to one breakdown at a time, please? If we all lose it at once, we're dead. The shadow stuff will suck out our souls, or whatever, and we'll get turned into more shadow."

"That sounds pretty concrete. How do you know all this? What else do you know that you're not telling us?" Rodolpho demanded as Matty fell into herself, dropping to her knees, hands over her face. The thing that wasn't her sister continued to call to her through the door. It sounded very close.

"I don't. I've just seen a bunch of horror movies. I don't know anything about this stuff in real life. My Gran might. Man, I wish she was here."

"Your 'Gran?' As in grandmother? That's who you'd want here facing off against a wall of darkness and something that disappeared over fifty people?" Rodolpho asked incredulously.

"She's one of the smartest, kindest, people I know, or have ever known," Nara said. "She's looked after me for nearly two decades, most of my life, got me through school, through a bunch of tests of life, like failed relationships, losing my parents... She always has a solution to my problems. She's stronger than steel. I'd take Gran over Superman, any day. Against ghosts and otherworldly stuff, doubly so," he finished, thinking of the altar he had found. Gran had to know something about all this. But he couldn't exactly go ask her right now.

"Then where is she now?"

"In the hospital. She had a... she had a weird kind of attack last night..."

"Did she turn into some kind of shadow beast?" Rodolpho asked. Nara's expression of disdain deepened.

"Come on, man, she had a heart attack or something. They're not really sure what it was, but now she's in a coma."

"Lois was in a coma for months before she slipped away, before my parents pulled the plug. The doctors said there wasn't any real brain activity, that she wasn't in there anymore. They didn't understand. They didn't know!"

"All right, we've got to block the door. You control her, keep her distracted or sit on her or something. I'm going to move the couch," Nara said. Working as shift manager at the coffee shop had helped him develop his telling-people-to-do-things voice. Another thing he owed his Gran.

"Come on, Matty, why don't you do a report? From deep inside the big scoop of the day. Get it before anyone else can, right?" Rodolpho said, backing away and swinging the camera toward the outer wall of the building so that Matty might move to stay in the frame. She must have been peeking through her fingers, because she immediately dropped her hands and stood, following the area before the camera, trying to place herself in its view.

$$\{\,7\,\}$$

"Matty!" The young woman's voice seemed to come from just outside the door now, even as Nara eased the couch into place against it. Something knocked. Goosebumps rose along Nara's arms, though which of the sounds, voice or rapping, really triggered it, he couldn't say.

"Don't listen to it!" Nara urged quietly. "Do your report, make your big contribution, get your pats on the back and big corner office," he said. Matty kicked over the bag he'd packed for Gran in her disorganized, sporadic movement through where the couch had been. The envelope fell out, but from it didn't spill cash. A small, dark object that looked vaguely like a top rolled onto the carpet. He picked it up.

As soon as his skin touched the smooth, glassy surface, Nara could see even more clearly through the darkness. A vague shadow of the outside world appeared through the windows. Red and blue lights flashed against window frames. A low whine came to his ears. It was steady, not a siren, but seemed to come from somewhere above. The thing on the other side of the door hissed as Matty stood by the window.

"Matty Stephens, Action Eye News, channel 113, on the scene at what must be the strangest event anyone in the collected emergency services of the city has ever witnessed. I now stand on the third floor of the apartment building at the corner of Chamberlain and 10th. It has been cut off from the outside world for nearly..." She checked her watch, a small gold affair with a white face and narrow, needle-like hands. "Ten hours now. The windows, as you can see, are covered from within by a black kind of shadow mist. As you'll see later in our exclusive report, and the follow-up special, this mist has been arranging itself into historical moments involving the tenants through the decades, especially terrible scenes, by and large. Meanwhile, there are no signs whatsoever of the more recent inhabitants of this corner of the 200 block. Many apartment doors stand open, dishes left on tables, phones and books dropped beside chairs as if something compelled these people out of the safety of their homes we know not where."

While Matty spoke, the object from the envelope hummed in Nara's hand. In the distance, he thought he heard rain pattering on a window, or maybe into a calm sea. A feeling of floating, bobbing slowly in the ocean, and being pulled along by a current enveloped him. He looked at the door. He hadn't heard anything from the voice that had been trying to lure Matty out since just after he had picked up the object.

He looked down at it again, a few narrow bands of silver and gold around the wider part of the teardrop shape and other colors near either end. Between was a mishmash of irregular shapes, each of different greens, blues, pinks, browns, yellows and more. They seemed to shimmer and shift as he watched, mesmerizing him. His hand rose, drifting toward the hallway.

"We've got to go," Nara said, waving Matty to wrap up her segment. He'd shifted the couch again while she spoke, barely drawing a glance from the woman as she pressed on, ever the professional. He picked up Gran's tote and took another step forward. "It's gone, the voice. I think this thing scared it away. We've got to go up."

"Ah yes, local business man Narayan Leon," Matty jumped into interview mode.

"Cut, Rodolpho, we've got to go while we can," Nara jumped in.

"You don't say 'cut.' *I* say 'cut,'" Matty snapped, all puffy eyes and nostrils wide.

"Well, I've got to go. This thing is practically pulling me toward the door, and the creature ran from it, so I figure that's a double win. If you want to stay here and shuffle deck chairs while the Titanic sinks, that's on you, but I'm following this... teardrop?" Nara said, not certain why he was being so insistent. Was it the object itself? Pushing him? Bending him to its will like a golden ring made by an evil wizard?

"Go then. This is what *we* came here for, to get the scoop, see the inside of this place before any other news source. Roll it, Rodolpho," Matty insisted. The man looked at his boss, then at Nara, then shrugged and settled his stance, half-sitting on the back of the returned couch.

"I hope you'll be all right, but I can't just sit here. I came here for a reason, too, and I'm going to check on my friend." He hesitated at the door, steeling himself, then pulled it open. The deeper dark had indeed fled, and he saw as he moved that even the wispier darkness pushed away from him as he walked with the teardrop shaped talisman in front of him. He could almost discern a sphere of clarity around him.

At the stairs, he blew out a rough breath and started up them, fairly certain that this was the way the creature had come from and likely fled to. Would it keep fleeing if he came across it again? Or was he backing it into a corner, forcing it to fight?

"Narayan!" He heard his name in his father's voice calling, distant, drawn out as though the man, years dead, was searching for him. Another trick. The creature was trying to get into his head, make him charge in blindly or run away. He resolved to do neither, at least until he had saved Carmen or verified he was gone. The mysterious talisman hummed in his hand now, pulling him in the direction of the voice.

What if this was a trap? What if someone delivered the thing to lure him here? Or to lure Gran? The latter thought curled his free hand into a fist. What did she have to do with this? Or was it all a big coincidence? That seemed unlikely.

Up the last flight to Carmen's floor, Nara took each step slowly, cautiously.

"Nara!" Tio Sylvester's voice.

"Narito!" Tio Tito. Eyes filling with tears, he stood at the top of the stairs, just outside the open door into the hallway, listening as best he could past the thumping of his heart. Thinking sneaky thoughts, clinging to the wall, Nara stepped through the doorway and made for Carmen's apartment, 808. Shadows swirled and formed faces which exploded against the barrier the charm created around him, disturbing him in their own way. He hunched to keep as much of his body inside the sphere as possible.

Nara realized he was going to have to leave the perceived safety of the wall and cross the hallway or spend precious minutes going halfway around the building. He took a deep breath, focused on the shape of a doorway in the opposite wall, and launched himself forward. He stumbled over something, feet leaving the floor, hands reaching into the darkness, seeking the wall to catch himself, but he only fell, spinning into the shadows.

{ **8** }

"Carmen!" He cried out, though he wasn't even sure the other man was still in the building or alive... Nara heard vicious, powerful rain drumming from every direction like he was in a metal-roofed, metal-walled shack. He collided with something in the dark. He flinched, pulling his hands back toward him and felt himself start to spin in the opposite direction. Meanwhile, something wooden sounding tapped against another such something, creating a cascade of rapping and knocking.

In his clenched fist, the teardrop began to glow. The light escaped between his fingers, showing the blocks and bands of color even through his flesh. He opened his hand a bit and the light streamed out, filling the space. He saw walls and the ceiling crisscrossed with strands of shadow, which drew together in the corners. Still he spun, and a moment later, the source of the clacking, which had all but faded, panned into sight.

He screamed, eyes bulging from his head. He clamped his fingers over the talisman again, but the mummified bodies of Carmen's neighbors still drifted in his mind's eye. He knew they would haunt his dreams forever, reaching hands curled into claws, clothes billowing away from diminished bodies. They had been dried out, drained perhaps. Rodolpho's suggestion about vampires didn't seem so far from the mark now.

Nara wondered where he was. It seemed clear this wasn't the hallway, or even an apartment in Carmen's building. Rain continued to tap in a chaotic rhythm, seemingly from every direction. A new sound came to his searching ears. It was a swishing of cloth, like a drape rustling in the wind or a shroud sliding over a body. A faint metallic ring followed, and panic flooded through him, speeding his heart again.

He tried to swim through the void, but where would he even go? He had to look again. Wincing, he opened his hand. The particolor glow, rooted in the brilliant sapphire light from the object's core, stabbed out into the space like a rainbow of swords. Colored spots of light played over dull gray walls, interrupted by bands and blots of black. The slithering something shifted quicker.

Eyes darting around, Nara took in as much of the room as he could, trying not to focus on the slowly twisting and rolling bodies. Was that a door? How was there still not a floor? Perhaps it was covered entirely with the nearly tangible shadows? Holding the teardrop between his thumb and forefinger, he swept it in the direction of the peaked ceiling.

Countless shadowy reflections of himself appeared as one across the expanse, moving as he moved, but then began to move over one another, some winking out as others eclipsed them.

"I wish I had more light," he muttered, patting his pockets for anything he might be carrying that could help. He wasn't in the habit of carrying a flashlight or even a lighter and found nothing of use. After a moment, though, a faint glimmer did creep along the walls, sparse like stars but sinister. The faint lights spread across the surface he took to be the floor. This shift did not encourage him. A pale light spread from one side, like dawn. For each of four glittering crescents of light maintaining relative position to one another, a shadowy body appeared in the new glow: round, hairy, and replete with limbs. Spiders!

"You've woken my pets," a voice whispered , slithering through his consciousness. "I've just managed to get them to sleep after their feed. I suppose they can have dessert..." A shadow lunged, separating from the rest. Downward curved blades glinted in the light of his talisman, extending from black sleeves of seemingly empty robes. A pale face flickered within the hood. The flickering itself reminded him of something he had only half seen. When Carmen was casting spells or whatever over Gran, the lights had flickered. A figure he hadn't entirely registered had stood in one of the suddenly dark doorways.

Flickering, Nara thought to himself. He took the teardrop into the center of his hand and punched out, causing light to flare from within it. The light revealed hundreds of spiders in their fullness, turning his stomach to ice, making his legs weak. The robed figure before him seemed solid. Beyond it, he saw the door. He grabbed a sleeve of the robe and hauled himself forward. Metal blades slashed at the air, shedding black sparks as they struck some invisible barrier.

He felt a tug at his center, something pulling him backward, but then he was through the door.

He fell onto his hands and knees, the teardrop bouncing away across threadbare carpet. Darkness collapsed around him like a blanket settling. Nails, or blades, scratched against the door behind him. He lunged forward, getting a finger on the glass trinket before it rolled farther away, coming to rest against the baseboard of the wall. The door splintered. He imagined a long, curved blade stabbing through. The sound of hundreds of tiny feet tapping leaked through from where he had been. Something sliced the air, and he felt his shirt pull and cool air caress his back. Scrambling, he recovered the teardrop, shifting his perceptions again. The door across the way looked intact.

The darkened hallway was empty of everything but stratified shadows and a susurrus of countless voices whispering. He stood, feeling his back for any sign of blood. The shirt was cut, but his body seemed intact. Orienting himself for a moment, he walked gingerly along the wall as if any step might break the floor and send him back to face the army of fist-sized spiders. Or maybe they had just been farther away and *seemed* that small... He shivered at the thought.

At Carmen's door, he knocked a pattern from pure habit, then, eyes wide, crouched against the door, scanning the darkness and listening hard for approaching danger. He put his hand on the door to steady himself as it swung inward freely. Expecting it to support him, he lost his balance, dumping himself into the apartment's front hall.

Rolling to his feet quickly, Nara stood looking at pen and ink drawings he'd seen thousands of times, landscapes depicting not-quite real places. Most were impossible-looking towers or irregular bridges. None of these were of the sea, but there was a common aesthetic that reminded him of his run in with the rainbow serpent. Was this where those strange visions had come from? Memories of Carmen's art? Or had Carmen seen similar things?

Trees were gnarled, ancient, magical-looking, nothing like those in the park. He gathered up the spilled book and sweater and stuffed them back into Gran's bag. Why was he even carrying this still? He couldn't put a finger on it, but it seemed important, like his last link to her.

"Carmen?" Nara called into the darkness. No answer. Here, the shadows hung thicker in the air, but there were still bands like strata in the walls of the Grand Canyon. He wondered vaguely about the varying weight of darkness as he crept along the right wall, finding the kitchen empty.

The living room took up the center of the apartment; a low coffee table, dark wood with stains and a plate with a few stray noodles, the couch from which Nara had watched more movies than he could remember, sitting between Carmen and Gran, empty now. The bathroom on the right, décor in nautical theme, empty. Next came the smaller bedroom Nara himself used when Gran went on trips to places he couldn't go, or she didn't think he'd have fun as a child, like Las Vegas.

Back across the way, Carmen's bedroom. He thought he smelled something, smoke? It grew stronger as he neared the door.

"Tio Carmen?" Nara said quietly at the door. There was no answer. Why would there be? No doubt he had heard voices of his loved ones trying to lure him out all night. Either Carmen was gone, or he knew the danger and was ignoring said voices.

Nara wracked his tired brain. What could he say to let the man know it was really him and not some spirit or demon? Something came to him. It seemed silly. He was embarrassed but cleared his throat and, deeply aware of his own lack of musical talent, began to sing in light voice, "Estrellita donde estás, quiero verte... titilar..."

{ 9 }

"Nara?" The man answered. "How did you- why are you- What?" The man was confounded. Seconds stretched.

"It was the first thing I could think of that no spirit was likely to know... The song you sang to me when I first came to live at Gran's."

"Certainly no spirit would murder that tune in quite the way you do..." The handle turned and the door opened just wide enough for him to see one of Carmen's brown eyes peering out at him. "It *is* you! Where is Aizah? She shouldn't have dragged you into this. We agreed ages ago." The door opened more fully, revealing Carmen in just a pair of flannel pants. His chest and arms were covered in black scrawlings. The room behind him was devoid of shadow, full of candles and small brass pots like the one he had seen in Gran's cabinet, and crystals catching the light and throwing tiny rainbows across the room.

"Into *what?* You *know* what's going on here?" Nara said, disbelieving.

"We're under attack, the whole... family... Is your Gran not here?"

"She's in the hospital. Had some kind of attack. You came to visit her... Did some kind of... spell over her? With sparkly dust?" Carmen stared, clueless. "She's in a coma, or was when I had to leave the hospital last night. They didn't call me, so I guess that's probably a good sign."

"Aizah being incapacitated explains some things. Talk about taking advantage of opportunities..." Carmen sighed.

"What opportunities? What is this all about? How do you not remember being in her hospital room."

"Sobrino mio... It would take way too long to explain, even if I was a hundred percent sure. Come in, tell me how you made it all the way here. No, wait, start earlier than that. Tell me about this 'attack' su abuela suffered." Carmen took a step back, allowing Nara into his sanctum. Nara sat in a chair in the corner while Carmen took turns pacing down a narrow lane between candles and incense holders and sitting at the corner of his bed, listening to Nara's tale with a serious look on his face.

"So what do we do now? Are we safe here?"

"For now, but I only have so much incense and coffee, and if I sleep, my protective spells will fail. The shadows will break through my defenses, and we'll be drained."

"Drained? So this *is* vampires?" Carmen laughed, a harsh, singular bark.

"No, sobrino, vampires are not a thing... well, they are, but nothing like the movies, and nothing like this. This is all pure natural order of the world stuff. We've got to get to Aizah."

"Can you help her with this stuff?"

"Estas cosas? No, I need to find a thing, a very special thing like a glass teardrop with lots of colored bits."

"This?" Nara fished the teardropfrom his pocket, where he'd put it when he had started trying to talk to Carmen through the door.

"Where en el infierno did you get that?"

"Someone left it, in an envelope. I thought it was rent at first."

"That's worth far more than rent. Do you have the envelope?"

"Uh, yeah, it's in the bag... I packed some stuff to bring to Gran in the hospital. A sweater, the book she was reading, you know."

"You're a good grandson. Aizah's lucky to have you."

"Um... thanks. Here." Nara found the yellow paper envelope. It didn't seem to have any writing on it. He held it out to the baker, but the older man didn't take it.

"It's probably better that I don't touch it. The fewer impressions on it the better if we're going to track down the one who brought you the gota. This kind of thing doesn't just get passed around like a desk fountain at a Yankee swap. Someone had a very compelling reason to leave this with you, or more likely, Aizah."

"Would it have kept her safe from the attack? Could it help her now?"

"Shhh!" Carmen hissed. The man stood, eyes closed, hands cupped together in a dome over the gota envelope. "Yes to the first, I don't know to the second. Get ready to light el sobre in one of the candles and then drop it in the bowl on the floor." He continued speaking or, at least, uttering syllables, but none of them made sense to Nara. The rhythm of them, though, reminded him of his exhaustion, lulling him into a trance-like state. He imagined things swimming around in the shadows in the hallway, all of the hallways, as though he could see them right through the walls. Two floors below, he saw Matty and Rodolpho. Finally, Carmen stopped and said, "Fuego! Ahora!" The words snapped him out of his reverie, and he turned, bathing the edge of the yellow paper in candle flame until it took, then bending to drop it into the brass bowl.

Ethereal trails rose up, writhing and shifting as regular smoke, but perhaps with a bit more purpose and much more cohesion. The pillar thickened and darkened but remained a medium gray. It reminded Nara of a snake rising up from a basket to the music of a flute.

"Ready?" Carmen asked, then swiped a toe across a line of powder at the door.

"Ready for what?" Nara replied. The smoke serpent sailed through the air and over the threshold, then made for the front door of the apartment.

"Bring the gota," Carmen said needlessly as he threw a backpack over one shoulder and followed the magical tracker. He had just said it was powerful, important, and might be able to save Gran. Nara wasn't letting something like that go without a fight.

"What is this thing? What is this all about? What does it have to do with Gran? Or all the people in this building?" he asked as he followed Carmen down the hallway. The other man just waved his hand behind him as though batting the questions out of the air.

The smudge of gray slithered through the shadows like a stray paint stroke. Nara held the gota in his hand, sensing its vibrations and pull that seemed aimed in the same general direction as the tracking... spell? Was this magic? What else? He chided himself. But how?

Carmen crept along with amazing stealth for an older man with a belly. His bare feet were probably an advantage, though Nara wouldn't have made that choice himself. At a corner, the baker stopped to look back, checking on Nara.

"Put that away. It'll attract more attention than we want right now."

"But it clears the air around us. Like your room."

"Exactly. You can't wave something like that around and not expect someone to notice. Just put it in your pocket for now. I think we're almost there. I didn't expect it to be such a short strip."

"Where is 'there?' Short trip?"

"That hallway is a dead end. Unless the seeking serpent is taking us down the fire escape, the culprit is in one of these four rooms."

"'Culprit?' Are we in a seventies cop show?"

"Shh," Carmen admonished. They watched the serpent slide through a door with "820" marked on it in brass numerals on peeling black stickers.

"What do we do now?" Nara asked. Carmen just waved at him to be quiet and crept forward, gaze locked on the door to apartment 820. Rolling his eyes, Nara followed. He fished around in his pocket for the gota.

The door suddenly opened inward, showing utter blackness which plumed outward as it had on the lower floor, now engulfing Carmen. Nara thrust the gota forward. As expected, the darkness peeled back under the sphere of force the object emitted against the shadow. What Nara didn't expect was what the receding darkness revealed. Carmen was no longer the affable, portly, baker he had known since he was small. The creature standing there in maroon plaid pajama pants, and nothing else, was a caricature of humanity.

Its limbs were long and thin, its muscles bunched knobs rather than gradual swellings, like a rough, early version of a clay statue, laying out the bulges and bumps, but none of the smooth outlines of a finished sculpt. Unfinished, yes, that was the impression that blossomed in Nara's brain. With the cracks at the joints, and across some of the broad surfaces, Carmen, or whatever was pretending to be Carmen, resembled a clay sculpture that had been roughed out, but then baked prematurely, locking him into some kind of primordial state.

Primordial Carmen turned toward Nara. Its cheekbones and chin thrust out in disturbing ways, like something was about to burst forth from the yellow-gray flesh. Its mouth was a jagged slash filled with haphazard teeth of varied direction and size. Its tongue rolled in its mouth like two serpents fighting, but before any sound could come from that hell-pit, Nara stumbled backward, taking the gota with him. The darkness crashed back in, hiding the creature from sight.

{ 10 }

F ist tight around the mystical gota, Nara rolled over and started crawling, then managed to regain his feet. He was halfway to the corner before he heard Carmen's voice behind him.

"¡Espera! I can explain!" the creature said in an all-too perfect mimicry of the man he had known most of his life. Nara rounded the corner, coming face-to-mass with a roiling cloud of deepest shadow. He held out the gota, trying to force the thing back. The storm of darkness poured over him. The gota held its ground, creating a spherical barrier around him, but still, the swirling, churning shadow engulfed that sphere, blocking out the hallway in a matter of seconds.

The gota itself glowed, dimly at first, a mere trickle of light between his fingers, but when he opened his hand, the radiance intensified again, splitting into rays from its core, taking on the deep blue of the core crystal and other colors as it struck the overlaid bands, squares, and irregular shapes in myriad colors.

"How am I going to get out of this?" Nara asked. Seemingly in response, the gota flashed suddenly brighter, blinding him.

***

Something grazed Nara's hand. He flinched, but then felt the soft, damp, warm breeze on his face, and more taps on his back and shoulder. His eyes adjusted, and he saw that he stood in a field of tall grass. The sky above him was thickly populated by clouds, some friendly and fluffy, others more threatening and gray. "Where am I now?" he asked no one. The grass was so high, so dense, he couldn't see ten feet in any direction.

"Can't just stand here." He began walking, carefully at first, pushing the grasses down with his foot before taking a step forward. This quickly grew tiresome, and he didn't find any soft spots or holes, so he began to tromp, reminding himself of the "giant game" Gran used to play with him. It had taken many forms: hide and go seek, chase or tag, tall-tale telling, even eating competitions to get him to finish his dinner, or holding his breath challenges to get him to get under the water in the bath to wash his hair. Here, it was the exaggerated stomping she would do to incite him to run in mock fear through the park.

Something low and dark emerged from the screen of tall, green stalks. Gradually, as he neared with more caution, he saw it was a rough stone wall. The stones were overgrown with lichen and moss and had no mortar that he could see. It was chest-high and enclosed a vast, but closely cropped, lawn with a small wood house on a stone foundation at the end of a stone walkway. Beside it was a garden and a row of trees. Excited by this find, something finally that wasn't terribly frightening, if still inexplicable, Nara walked along the wall, looking for a gate or opening. After some time, the clouds above darkening, he stopped.

"This isn't getting me anywhere. I need to get in there."

Stuffing the gota back in his pocket, he climbed over the ancient wall full of footholds and handholds. He rolled off, falling to the grass on the other side. Walking toward the house, he noticed outbuildings in the distance. The sky rumbled, shaking his chest, and he began to run. The wind picked up, blowing his hair and setting the trees to dancing. The house didn't seem to be getting any closer. He ran on. Fat drops of rain began to fall, their strikes reverberating through the ground to his feet, not a patter, but a barrage. He poured on the speed.

Again, the drops brought flashes of memory, warehouses and workshops, mines and markets, people working and shopping, traveling by foot, horse, or car... They became a blur, but one that hummed through his whole body with sensations of heat and cold, bright days and dark nights. It became difficult to pick out the small house before him in the flickers between.

Achingly slowly, the house grew nearer. It didn't take long to realize that it wasn't a quaint little house in the middle of a field. It was oversized, the foundation of boulders the size of normal houses, the boards from ancient trees as massive as redwoods. The edge of the low porch across the front of the building, which would normally have been an easy step up, was an overhang affording him cover from the rain without even crouching down.

Between the inchoate drumming of rain drops that could have filled a swimming pool in seconds, Nara heard something else, a drag and thump that reverberated through the wooden porch boards. A tone rang out, cutting across the thud of rain and what Nara feared were footsteps. Why would there be a giant house if there was no giant? He looked at the gap between the beam supporting the front of the porch and the ground. He could fit, if he had to...

The tone shifted, then again, becoming a tune.

Whistling. The giant is whistling, he realized. He hoped that it meant the creature was in a good mood. Whatever its disposition, Nara felt reconnaissance was necessary. He reached up to the edge of the porch and, shoving off from one of the rough pillars supporting the porch roof, managed to heave himself up. The door was like the illustrations from fairy tale books, unlike anything he'd seen in person, a few vertical boards and a rectangular handle he assumed would lever down or up to allow one to open the door. But he wouldn't be heavy enough to budge it with all his weight, let alone heave open the door, even if he could get up there. He would have to find another way in.

After minutes of searching, Nara found a gap where wood met stone. Climbing into it, he could see the structure of the wall and places where the mud had not fully sealed the spaces between boards. He pushed through and came out into a corner behind a stand of split logs. As he stood, trying to orient himself, one of the massive wedges of wood rose into the air. Nara ducked behind the stand but peered out to observe the giant that emerged.

A woman, vaguely familiar, with brown hair tucked under a kerchief, deeply tanned arms and face, had the beginnings of lines around her features. She shoved the log into a massive stone fireplace and stirred a blackened metal pot. This *was* just like a fairy tale. He just had to be sure not to end up in the pot.

"You be good," the giantess boomed. "Mama's just going to get some veggies from the garden. I'll be right back." The floor shook again as the creature walked to the door, picked up a basket, and exited. The door slamming was enough to knock Nara from his perch. He landed with a thump, flat on his back, he lay there, stunned, for long seconds. When he recovered, he peered around the corner of the black metal wood rack.

A child the size of a small house sat on the floor, playing with wooden animals and people. She cooed and hopped the figures around in approximations of them walking, content to play by herself, not seeming to notice her mother had gone.

"Hello, little one," she said, not looking up. *Little One,* just what Gran called him well after he towered over her. When had she stopped? He couldn't quite remember, but it seemed unimportant at the moment. "You don't have to be afraid. We giants don't bother eating such small creatures." Reassuring? He wasn't so sure, even if that was the girl's intent. "Do you want to come play for a while? It's stormy out there. That's why I have a house, for when it's dark and scary out."

Accepting that she clearly knew he was there, and not seeing a way for him to escape if she did mean him harm, he stepped out from behind the wood stack.

"What's your name?"

"Narayan," he said slowly. His was not a common name in the US. He had only seen it in books from other places.

"That's a lovely name. Mine's-" The front door slammed open, and the soaked giantess stomped in carrying a literal truckload of giant carrots, radishes, and tomatoes. Nara barely stayed on his feet due to the accompanying tremors.

"Ah! What's that?" the giant woman screamed, dropping her basket. Vegetables bounced and launched toward him, rolling at him like cars on a freeway. Everything was moving so fast, Nara panicked, running instinctively toward the seeming safety of the stone hearth. A tomato struck him, knocking down and sending him rolling across the floor. His shirt caught on a splinter at the edge of a board, jerking him to a stop as the world went black.

{ 11 }

"Lo siento, niño, that had to be rough. It's over now." Carmen was the speaker, his back to Nara who found himself lying in a bed.

"Where am I? What are you?" Nara asked.

"Now that second one's a big, tangled-up question. Let's tackle the first. You're in apartment 820, the home of the traitor."

"Traitor?"

"Apparently. I thought she was dead, but then..." Carmen waved a distorted hand, extending extra-long fingers sprouting directly from his wrist. The effect gave Nara a shiver. The room was not unlike the spiritual bunker Carmen had made in his own apartment. Candles and incense sticks stood all around. Small bundles of bones and feathers hung at the center of designs painted on the walls and ceiling. Red and black and yellow were common colors, forming a theme, even to a brass bowl supported by polished black and red pillars with yellow-painted symbols etched into each one. "The Plumber came here looking for the gota, thinking the traitor must have had it, and she did... until... they tried to throw your Gran debajo del autobús."

"What did you do with Carmen? Are you going to eat me, too?" The creature chuckled, shaking its head and continuing to do whatever it was it was doing, dropping things into the larger brass bowl. Sparks flew. Smoke wafted. The sound of rain rose and then fell away. An astringent smell stung Nara's eyes and nose. Tears welled up.

"I *am* Carmen, the same Carmen you've known since you were four. I didn't possess him, or eat him, or anything like that. This is me, just as I've always been. Well, as I've been since long before you were born, anyway. It's a long story."

"And Gran is part of that story?"

"A large part, yes. Ideally, she would tell it to you. If we can save her, maybe she will."

"Save her? From the traitor?"

"No, I don't think so. Why would she attack her and also deliver the means to save her? There's something deeper going on here than even I understand. Something to do with the Plumbers."

"Did you say 'plumbers' again? Like guys who work on your toilet?"

"I prefer the bathtub or basin analogy, but if you must, sure."

"That doesn't really explain anything." Carmen shrugged, focusing on whatever he was doing. Nara heard something that sounded like pebbles fall into the bowl. The metal rang, then there was a dragging sound, as though Carmen was stirring the ingredients.

"So what are you doing?" Nara asked, looking around the room for a weapon or means of escape. The door looked normal. He didn't see a lock. But where would it lead? He remembered the apartment that had turned out to be a room full of floating corpses and hungry spiders. He shivered.

"Trying to understand."

"So am I. What happened to Gran? Who did it? If not the traitor, then these Plumbers? Why? What are you? How come you look different since the shadow cloud stuff?" Carmen groaned and turned toward Nara.

"You're not going to let me just work, are you? This is like the museum all over again. 'Where are the monkeys?' 'Where are the monkeys?' Like it was the zoo…"

"You know about that?"

"Who else would, sobrito? It was just you and me that day, and I'm not big into posting my entire life on social media."

"I'm not asking you to tell the world. I'm just asking you to tell *me*. What is going on?" Carmen sighed and grabbed the chair tucked into the desk he was standing over. He settled onto it backward, knees out at angles, arms folded across the top of the back.

"All right, fine, but if su abuela asks, you did your own research, poking around in the weird corners of the interwebs and such."

"Ok, whatever. I just need to know. I mean, look at me, I'm neck deep in it anyway, aren't I?"

"That you are, sobrito. That you are. The first thing you gotta know is that there is an afterlife, a place you go when you die, and it's nothing like any book you read or movie you see... It's like... You know in science class they talk about how all life came from the sea? The primodial ooze or whatever? A big guiso, a stew of all the chemicals life needed to do its thing and start evolving? It's a lot like that, a big sea of energy, ideas, dreams-"

"Rainbow snakes and giants and rain..." Nara said off hand, relating things he had recently dreamed about. Carmen raised a ridged eyebrow.

"Yes, exactly. The rain is like... This is where the metaphors get a little mixed up, but reality, it's never so cut and dry as a story, right? Hold the rain for a minute. We'll get back around to it. Now, this world, the living world, is full of creatures having experiences, learning, loving, hurting, winning and losing, inventing. People, especially humans that is, *love* creating. Painting, drawing, singing, sculpting, architecture... That's how we ended up with all this stuff all over the place... Uh, anyway," he said, realizing he'd started veering off track. "These experiences kind of build up inside you, your memories and everything, like water filling a tub. The more you live your life, the fuller that tub gets, and the bigger, richer, your soul is when your plug gets pulled."

"When you die," Nara said.

"Exactamente," Carmen pointed a disturbingly long finger at Nara, "and now we go back to the rain. When you die, those experiences and energies, you built up over your life, drop *down* into the next place. There's a reason some people call it the 'underworld'. All those energies and experiences, the spirits, if you will, kind of fall down into this big ocean. They mix and react and evolve into a whole new world, or maybe you could say a bunch of different worlds, as certain kinds of energies stick together and build up islands in the primodial sea."

"Wow, that's... I mean, that's a neat take on what could be after this, but what does any of it have to do with Gran? With you?" Nara asked.

"Well, if there's one thing that people strive for more than emotional connection and creating things, it's más."

"'More?'"

"Sí, más de todo, más money, más food, más good experiences, más tiempo. More *life*. Immortality. Even knowing there's something in the next world, that some form of who we are persists, no one wants to change, not like that. It's a big gamble, splitting up into thousands of pieces. And most people are pretty attached to who they are, how they envision themselves, anyway. They don't want to get all mingled together with other souls and form a new being, especially if that means forgetting who they are, or... *being* forgotten." The building creaked around them. Nara's ears popped.

"Something's happening," he said, looking at the door again.

"I can feel it, too. I thought this was just a trap for me, to keep me here, unable to help Aizah, but it could be there's something more, something... We've got to get you out of here. Take the gota with you. I've done what I can with it to try to unbind myself from this place, to let me escape, but we're out of time."

"What about this traitor? What did she do?" Nara pressed, "Come on, Carmen. Estoy a oscuras. You're the only one who can shed some light."

"Fine," Carmen agreed with another sigh, "What do you want to know?"

"Not want, *need*. You've been a part of... whatever this is for longer than I've been alive, and I'm just hearing about it now. I've got a lot of catching up to do if I'm going to survive..." He waved a hand around to indicate the whole situation. "This."

"You're right. You're probably old enough to learn the truth."

"The traitor?" A low whistling sound, like wind through trees in winter, issued from somewhere outside of the room.

"Had to start at the hardest part, didn't you, sobrino?" Carmen said evasively. Nara stared, meeting the monstrous gaze of the creature he was having trouble thinking of as his tio. "Fine. Your Gran, your whole family really, your blood family, were the core of this group... Not really a religion, but with their own -our own- ideas about how life, and death, should be."

"'Not a religion' but kind of like a religion, so... a cult?" Nara asked.

"We don't use that word, but it could be argued," Carmen allowed, "during an important rite, one of us, I think there were about fifty of us at the time, one of us... went rogue. I figure she must have been turned by the Plumbers. She tipped them off as to where we would be, where *this* was." Carmen held up the gota, cradled in the distorted digits of his hand. "We weren't hurting anyone. We just wanted more years, as I said. Aizah had found ways to take more years, to keep dancing and singing and... living."

"So you were attacked?"

"Sí.

{ 12 }

"And Gran? Is Gran immortal?" Nara asked, his heart in his throat. Could it be true? What did it mean for her recovery? For him?

"After a fashion, though it sounds like the Plumbers are trying to get to her drain."

"Immortality is keeping your soul from going down the drain? That kind of puts a weird perspective on life."

"Don't I know it, sobrito. Go, back the way you came before it's too late."

"I don't know if I can. The tunnel is coming apart."

"You came in by the tunnel under the street? If it's not blocked off... there's a chance... All right, we'll do this together, if we can. You might have just saved me, after all, niño." Carmen grabbed some red and black stones and put them inside the brass bowl with a few other objects, then dropped them in Gran's tote and shoved them into Nara's arms. "You carry this stuff. I'm going to need my hands free." The creature held up his creepy all-fingers hand, revealing the gota, which seemed somehow more intense now. The building groaned again. Somewhere nearby, windows shattered. Carmen pressed the talisman into Nara's hand.

"Corre!" Carmen said, dragging him out of the room. They stood in a living room. The apartment had the same layout as Carmen's but reversed. The windows exploded, raining glass into the room. Nara threw an arm up to shield his face and ran toward the kitchen, but Carmen hauled him into the hallway then ran for the stairs. The shadows bunched up and twisted into creature-like forms but seemed to be fighting to stabilize. Carmen ran right through something like a panther with too many legs, forcing it to dissipate. It had half reformed by the time Nara came to it. A claw solidified from the fog, catching his shirt, tearing through it with no effort and scoring a line of fiery pain across his ribs. Nara gasped.

As they descended, he could feel blood making rivulets down his side, soaking the waistband of his pants. Four flights later, he heard a scream and remembered Matty and Rodolpho.

"I wasn't alone. There was a reporter and her camera-man," Nara said.

"Really?"

"They paid me three bills to show them the way. Something about beating everyone else to the story."

"They're going to beat everyone else to después del mundo."

"We should save them." Carmen made a sound of disgust.

"No tenemos tiempo." A heavier crash from above reverberated through the building. "This place is coming down. Las sombras have been weakening the building's material connection to this world. The whole deal is about to get sucked into the afterworld."

"We have to try. At least lead them out."

"Fine. Rapidamente. We could have minutes... or seconds."

"Understood," Nara said, then yelled out into the darkness. "Matty! Rodolpho! Time to go!" He only heard crunching and a screeching wail in reply. Somewhere, the air was being sucked out of the building. That would only make it collapse faster. Nara ran to the apartment, where he'd left the pair.

"I'll, uh stay here. I don't have time to cast my disguise spell, and that energy might be better spent elsewhere soon."

"Right on. I'll be as quick as I can."

The living room was empty. Nara called out again.

"Here! We're here!" came the muffled cries from a closet. Nara pulled at the door, but it wouldn't budge. He put Gran's bag on the couch and took hold of the handle with both hands, setting a foot against the frame.

"The door's stuck. Help me with it. On three, you push, I'll pull!" Nara yelled through the wood panel. "One, two, three!" he counted, then hauled as hard as he could. He heard someone making an effort on the other side, saw the door bulge outward a little, but it didn't open. "Again, one! Two! Three!" Nara pulled with everything he had and launched away from the door, bouncing off the corner of the couch and falling to the carpet. The knob dropped out of his hands.

"Come on, sobrino!" Carmen called from the hallway.

"They're in the closet. The shifting weight of the building is like a vise on the door. The handle came off!" Nara called back.

"Dios mío..." Carmen muttered, coming into the room. He stepped over Nara, slid the long fingers of both hands under the door, and pulled. The wooden panel creaked and whined and finally cracked right up the middle, coming free in two larger pieces and dozens of smaller ones. Matty and Rodolpho stood before them stunned, their eyes wide.

Carmen dropped the free side of the door, while the other side swung weakly on its hinges. He waved the pair out, but they cowered in the back of the closet. "We've got to go. The building is collapsing. We're going to have words about you dragging my nephew into such a dangerous situation."

"Drag? Nephew? We followed him," Rodolpho said, spotting Nara getting up from the floor. "Carmen?" he asked, shaking off his shock. "Um, thanks for rescuing us. When the windows started exploding, we hid." Matty continued to stare.

"No time to explain or to argue, let's go," Carmen said, shoving Rodolpho toward the door and reaching for Matty. She squeaked and ran past her cameraman into the hall. Nara hopped over the couch, snagging the tote and following her.

***

The speakeasy was just a lonely storeroom once again. The shadows flowed toward the center of the building.

Nara wondered if that's where the creatures were, too, or the traitor Carmen had mentioned. So much still didn't make sense. None of it would, if they couldn't get back down the tunnel before the place collapsed into another realm.

The door to the tunnel was also still open. Nara could hear water as they neared, distinctly louder than before. That was not a good sign. His apprehension bore out as they started down the narrow passage. There was an active breeze now, right into their faces as the building behind them dragged everything toward its center like a black hole. Then they came to the gap in the floor.

"You jumped over *that* to get into the building? Should have put you in the Olympics," Carmen noted.

"We all made it, more or less," Rodolpho said, rubbing his scratched-up belly.

"Yeah, it was a lot narrower the first time. All the shaking from the building falling apart must have jostled it more," Nara said.

"Mmhm... and weakened the matter's bonds to itself and neighboring matter," Carmen agreed.

"So what do we do? We can't jump that, and we can't dig our way out. There wasn't anything we could make a bridge with."

"I've got an idea, but you're going to have to trust me," Carmen said.

"Not much choice at this point," Matty said. "What even are you? A zombie? A demon?"

"I'm going to need you all to stay frosty. No freaking out," Carmen said, ignoring Matty's questions.

"There's a category five tornado forming in the middle of a building I was just inside and am still way too close to. If I was going to freak out, I would have," the reporter argued. "You're not going to try to throw us across, are you? You're big, but you're not *that* big."

"Close, actually. I'm going to climb out over the middle, anchoring myself to the walls with my legs. My body and arms will be hanging down like in a circus act. Each one of you is going to run and jump. We'll catch hands and I'll swing you on to the other side."

"I... I don't see how that will work," Matty said.

"That's where the trust comes in," said Carmen. "Let's go."

"What about my camera? I can't hold onto it and do acrobat trapeze shit," Rodolpho said, eyeing the gaping hole in the floor.

"No worries," Carmen said, taking the camera from its harness on the man's chest and hurling it down the hallway over the crevice. It landed with a crash, bits of plastic and metal flying off, about ten feet past the far side of the hole.

"Hey! That equipment is worth thousands!" Rodolpho protested.

"Not to mention the footage we got!" Matty chimed in.

"The footage is fine. You can buy a new camera, not a new life. We have to go. Now!" Carmen spread his arms and legs wide. Matty screamed, the new pose striking up some primal fear hidden in the back of her mind.

"What the Hell *is* that?" Rodolpho framed his colleague's screams more coherently.

"That's mi tio, man, just be cool. He's our only way out of here, unless you want to try to medal in the long jump in the next fifteen seconds," Nara said. "Vamos!"

"Come on, Matty! We've gotta try!" Rodolpho said, moving back from the hole to get room to run. This forced Matty and Nara back toward the speakeasy. Wind screamed through broken windows and a series of crashes reinforced that there wasn't much time.

"You've got your head on. You go. Maybe when she sees it's all right, she'll snap out of it," Nara suggested. Rodolpho nodded and blew out a sharp breath, then ran for all he was worth toward the hole. As before, the edge crumbled beneath his foot as he tried to push off. He tumbled forward, arms wheeling. Carmen managed to catch one, but just one, flailing arm and they heard a sickening crack as the arm either broke or dislocated under the man's weight. Either way, he let out a pained yell and soared feet-first to the other side, slamming into the stone floor and skidding to a stop against the corpse of his beloved camera.

"All right, now you. If Carmen can get big, round, tall, Rodolpho across, you'll be no problem," Nara tried to reassure the woman. She nodded, but her eyes were glazed. He was losing her. Shock. Not unexpected, but in this case deadly. "Come on, let's run," he urged, putting a hand on her lower back and shoving her ahead of him. "Run! Run! Bear!" he called with increasing urgency, hoping to fool her confused mind into doing the one thing that could save her.

Finally, he had to stop, or try to jump alongside her, and he wasn't sure about Carmen's preparedness to deal with both of them at once, or the wall's ability to hold all that weight. Matty ran right off the edge of the hole and pitched forward, but Carmen was on his game and scooped her up, with long fingers under each arm. She swung forward, screaming again as she came face to face with the creature he'd grown up calling tio.

Matty landed flat on her back, bouncing slightly, and careening into Rodolpho, who still hadn't sat up. That was a problem for two minutes from now Nara told himself and nodded to his uncle. Remembering his Gran's bag, he stuffed the gota in his pocket once more and hurled the tote like a bowling ball. The bag arced up and landed right beside Rodolpho's head.

"Nice shot, sobrito. You were always good at bocce. Now you, before we get sucked into that vortex." Nara glanced over his shoulder and saw that the entire back wall had been stripped away by the pull of whatever was happening in the building. All he could see were swirling shadows and stones and debris from the tunnel starting to fall in. How far would it go? How long would it last? Was this the end of the world?

He shook his head and ran as fast as he could, bending his legs, pumping his arms, and launching a foot before the edge of the chasm to try to have decent footing. Instead, the whole section of floor gave way, creating a slide. He fell onto his back, slipping to the edge of the floor and out into the void.

"No!" Carmen yelled above him. Then Nara felt the other's bony grip around his leg, and he lost all sense of direction as he was swung through the darkness. He could hear the walls and floor crumbling, stone slamming against stone, rotten support beams against chunks of mortar, then the wall slammed into him.

$$\{\ 13\ \}$$

Nara came to on a broad expanse of bare wood. It was the first thing he saw as his eyes focused. The second was the child giant from before, sitting this time at a table that had seen better days, cobwebs clouding the underside and between the three unbroken legs. The last leg, a jagged stump dangling in the air, looked like something protruding from a cave ceiling.

There was other damage besides, dings and scratches and even some scorch marks he felt he would have noted before. And it wasn't just the table. The floor was marred and the walls. One of the window's panes was just a sad, little translucent tooth, while dust blew in around it, riffling torn and faded curtains.

He looked around, noting that the front door was just a simple rectangle now, the wall textureless and blank. What had happened here? Or was still happening?

"Excuse me," he said quietly to the girl at the desk. She had her head down on her folded arms.

"Hmm? Is someone there?" she asked, tears coloring her voice.

"It's me, Nara, down here."

"Oh, you again!" Her expression brightened, then faded to sadness again. "I'm afraid you haven't come at a very good time. Things are going wrong."

"I see that. What can I do to help?"

"We lived here for a very long time, a very, *very* long time... I came here whenever I was tired, or scared. But now... I can't seem to make it stay."

"I don't understand. I guess I'm not really sure where I am right now."

"Soon, too soon, this will be nowhere. The sea is rising, swallowing this little island. I could only hold it together with energy from above, the power of living, but now I've sprung a leak. I'm draining away."

"A Plumber?" Nara asked, recalling that Carmen had thrown the word around when explaining about filling and draining tubs. The girl nodded. "I always thought plumbers were the good guys."

"Most people do. I suppose it all depends on if you need a pipe to be clogged or flowing." While they spoke, the rain began again. Droplets struck the window shard, and it visibly melted a bit, its edge rounding, its point drooping. A crash made him jump. Turning instinctively, he saw the door had fallen in. It was wet on the upper face. He watched the grain fade and blur into a single color of brown. Beyond, he saw that the grass was a uniform green puddle. The house creaked much like Carmen's building had.

The last hours flooded back to him. The apartment building. Matty and Rodolpho and Carmen. He shivered.

"Sorry the fire's gone. It was one of the first things to fail. All those colors, the movement, it was so complex, so greedy," the girl said. "I'll be gone soon. Before the house, I should expect, though it won't last long without me. A house must be kept, no?" Nara nodded, uncertain what he should say. "Do you want to play? I still have a few toys... over there..." As the girl gestured to a pile of blocks, simple cubes, and rectangular prisms he recognized as the same colors as the carved animals and people from before, he felt a tug in his belly. He fell back a step, unbalanced, but then lifted into the air. "No, don't go! I'm so lonely now. It's almost over. I don't want to be alone..."

"I'm not doing this. Something... something's pulling me," Nara tried to reassure the girl. He flew backward toward the door. The girl stood, her features smooth and blank like an unpainted doll. She reached for him, but whatever force had him pulled hard just then, yanking him out of reach. He doubled over, his limbs flailing behind him like the tail of a kite.

In seconds, Nara soared through the sky, the giant farm fading down to a regular sized farm, then an ant farm, then a tiny speck in the middle of a sea of pale green. In between flashes of the countryside, he saw fragments of memories, people in churches, eating dinner at home, driving, so many moments driving and waiting. Each carried an emotion that shot through him like hot and cold flashes, boredom, regret, and joy at seeing someone again after a long absence, anger, fear...

As he got higher, he spotted what the girl had been saying. The edges of the field were jagged and ran right to broad, blue waves with no beach, no rocks visible. This seemed sad to him, the end of something. The end of the girl, perhaps. He barely knew her but felt as though he was losing something, too.

He spotted oddments as he had before, a gargantuan golden coin occupied by sapphire sea lions, all glittering and shining in sourceless light as rain poured down, a tracery of colored lines like wires in an electronic device, bundles splitting, recombining with other bundles, twisting up into a grove of rainbow trees dangling with square green leaves glittering with edges of silver and gold. It was all so different, but somehow familiar, like he could see how they came about, the logic behind them.

Clouds engulfed him. He tried to turn his head to see something, anything, but it was all gray and white and then nothing. Darkness followed.

***

Nara opened his eyes in a tunnel. His eyes took a moment to adjust to the daylight streaming in from the end of the stone-walled tube, only five feet away. Everything beyond that was a vast earthen bowl with sky visible above. Jagged pipes spewed water in falling arcs. He heard sirens in the near distance and people crying, screaming. He tried to sit up, but his body was wracked with pain. A helmeted head appeared above him, a silhouette against the bright blue of the sky.

"You all just stay still. We'll get you out of there as quickly as we can and see to your wounds," someone said over a speaker, their voice distorted, but largely understandable. Nara saw Matty and Rodolpho lying nearby, but there was no sign of Carmen. Had the man sacrificed himself to save him? It certainly seemed like it from the fuzzy memories he had of the jump across the gap. His mind returned to a riot of scraping, sliding, crunching rock, swinging through the dank air. The sound of water rushing faded like a receding wave as the world went gray around him.

"Yeah, not going... any..." he attempted to respond, slipping from consciousness.

***

Nara was vaguely aware of swaying, being lifted. He opened his eyes to the sea once more. A mountain made of waffles dominated one side, with at least three clusters of houses on its slopes, tiny, picturesque towns that struck a chord somewhere in his deep memory. A castle loomed farther up, and rivers of syrup cascaded down falls, collecting in small lakes. The light flickered, and he saw the mountain wreathed in shadows like those that had filled Carmen's apartment building.

They formed layers and encircled the mountain, which itself turned gray and sagged. He watched, transfixed, though he wanted to look away, to run. As he watched, some of the shadows coalesced into a long, thin, robed body with broad wings. It landed on the mountain, gripping one of the wide, square-pocked sides and pulling back. Beneath the surface lay a great, gray skull. Fear filled Nara's heart, and he recoiled into the clouds, losing sight of the terror.

{ 14 }

Nara was aware of a warmth, something hugging him tight. He tried to raise his arms to hug back, but everything was so heavy. He tried to take a deep breath but found he couldn't. The hugger was holding him too tightly. He struggled to open his eyes and found himself in a white room. A hospital. No, he was supposed to visit someone else in a hospital... Gran? Gran! He tried to sit but only gained a few degrees before his muscles betrayed him, and he flopped back against pillows.

"Ah, we caught a lively one. Just lay back for now. You'll get enough crunches in during rehab," a nurse smiled at him from the doorway.

"Gran... Aizah Leon..."

"Aizah... that name rings a bell. I'll check to see if any-one's tried to visit you yet..." The nurse vanished, leaving him alone with muddled thoughts and a dull floating sen-sation. He tried to assess his situation and found one arm in a cast, something binding his chest, and an IV in his other arm. Someone had placed a remote control near his unen-cumbered hand, but he only fumbled with it for long min-utes, failing to get it to come on before the nurse came back.

"I'm sorry hun, no one has come to visit you. Do you know your parents' numbers? Or anyone we can call?"

"My... Gran is here... a patient. My parents are... gone. Leon, Aizah..."

"Leon, you said. I'll check. Sounds like you've been having a hell of a week. I'll be right back." The lights flickered once, twice, then on the third, the room filled with sudden and complete shadow.

"Give it to me, and I'll let you live out your infinitesimal, insignificant life," something whispered to him in the dark. The voice reminded him of the creature from the room full of mummified bodies and the army of spiders.

"You make it sound so appealing," Nara said, trying to sound calm and brave, though he fought to find his voice. He had no idea how to deal with these things. Carmen had never gotten as far as explaining what they were, what they wanted, or how to send them packing. The other laughed; a raspy, mirthless sound that hung in the air like the stench of dead fish.

"You think you're saving her, but she's already finished. It won't be long now," the other hissed. "She's broken all the rules, and now, finally, after as many lifetimes as most of your kind get years, she'll come to an end as everything is meant to."

"You're a Plumber."

"If you like. You cannot hurt me with words any more than a gnat may insult a man."

"Then how *can* I hurt you?" Nara asked, eyes narrowing.

"You... are definitely Aizah's descendant. You know just enough of the law to flaunt it but not enough to understand its value, the order it creates. The living die. That is their lot. They build and grow and experience, then they seed the next world and all its realities. If you ignore that, if no one dies here, the next world dries up. The 'Plumbers,' as you so flippantly call us, are keepers of order, gardeners who tend the worlds and the flow of energies through the trophic levels. Despite your peoples' limited perceptions and understanding, the universe is not truly infinite. There is not endless energy."

"Thanks for the science lesson. I feel smarter already," Nara said, trying to rile the other.

"You are welcome. The greater everyone's understanding of their role, the more likely they are to choose to fulfill it."

"Whatever you say, breezy." Nara had been slowly working his hand down to his side. His pants were gone and with them, the gota. He sighed in disappointment. The presence seemed to recede then. Perhaps the Plumber knew he had had the gota, but could tell he didn't have it now, and was drawing back to look for it.

Reasoning the object must be in Gran's bag, on the chair a few feet away, Nara summoned all his strength and rolled in that direction. His leg flopped, numb, unreactive, immediately pulling him toward the floor. His broken arm bumped the lowered metal rails of the bed, sending a painful shock, which cut through the haze of a light concussion and medication.

With his free hand and one responsive leg, he pulled himself partway up and swung around, pushing through something with a vague, gauzy substance, but little resistance to his movement. He launched himself at the chair, not trusting himself to actually crawl, and slammed face-first into the corner of the stuffed square of the seat.

The brass bowl rang with the shifting of its contents. Chemicals and botanicals filled his nose and lungs, making his eyes water and forcing a cough. His good hand slapped white linoleum. His bad one struck the floor, jarring his whole arm and forcing a cry that welled up from deep in his throat. Tears streamed down his face. His legs dropped to the floor and he was able to pull himself forward, reaching up as darkness closed back in around him, the Plumber noticing his interest.

Nara reached up and rooted around in the bowl for the gota, eliciting scraping and ringing sounds. The air buzzed louder and louder as shadows crowded out every ray of light. For long seconds, fingers flitted blindly across bones and stones and leaves and cloth packets.

Finally, he found his jeans. Slipping a finger into the pocket, he touched something slick with faint bumps on the surface. Working his fingers under it, he grasped the crystal teardrop and the shadow retreated around him. He turned to sit with his back against the chair and saw a tangle of bones and shadow that was more like a child's macaroni art project, adorned with black spiderwebs, than a skeleton hovering a couple of feet away.

Bones sat edge beside edge and crossing over at odd points. They were mismatched in size and some, he was fairly sure, were upside down or backwards in their orientation. He couldn't help but laugh. When he did, the gota flashed with a bright light, and the creature and its shadowy fog fled.

"I said I was coming right back. You could have waited for whatever thing you needed from that bag of crazy." The nurse from minutes before stood in the doorway again, hands on her hips.

"I really couldn't." He said sharply, then, contrite, "Sorry, I just... I don't like being without it. It was in my pocket, but my pants are..."

"Yeah, that happens when you get yourself banged up in a dirty tunnel. There was blood and dirt and Lord knows what else all mashed into them. We had to cut them off you to examine you. Now back in bed. Don't make me get straps."

"Yes ma'am, sorry." Nara allowed the nurse to help him to the bed and leaned back but couldn't lay down without letting go of all control and flopping again.

"All right, hold on, you're going to hurt yourself all over again. Let me help you. There you go." She got an arm under him and helped him lay back.

"Thanks." Nara lay in his bed, tired, aching, the fright and adrenaline of the experience having focused him and burned off some of the pain medication in his system. All his body wanted to do now was sleep, but he had bigger needs. "Did you find Gran? With everything that's happened, I don't remember what room number she's in, but I brought her in myself," he said. "She raised me. She's the only family I have."

"I did find her on the list, room four one three, but I can't give you any kind of official update. I'll let her doctor know you're here, and maybe he can find time today to come see you. I'm sorry your family is going through this rough patch right now, but it will pass." The woman tilted her head and smiled a strange smile, her eyes full of memories, seeing something from her past rather than him. She reached out and lay her hand along his cheek. After a moment, she returned to herself, realizing what she had had done, and pulled her hand back. "I'm sorry. You... you just remind me of someone *I* lost a long time ago. I'll find that doctor," she said and all but ran out of the room.

{ 15 }

Had there been tears in her eyes? Was what was going on with Gran doing things to the people around her? He'd been having strange dreams. Carmen and his whole apartment building... The shadows in the room just now and the nurse? How were they all connected? Or were they connected at all? He remembered how the human mind's main strength was correlating things, from three spots that looked like a face, to reading, not one letter, or even word, but lines at a time, parsing them in not quite linear order...

A knock at the door drew Nara's attention.

"Hey, champ." Eli, who had worked at the coffee shop for over half of Nara's life and was like another uncle to him, smiled from the doorway. "Rough day. I heard Carmen's whole building is..." the man flung his hands up miming an explosion, then brought them back together in a clap.

"Yeah, it was scary. Carmen's... I think he's gone, Paulina and Gustavo and some others, too. I found Carmen... We, me and Matty and Rodolpho, almost got out. He *got* us out. Without him, we would have all been sucked into the next world. Game Over."

"Carmen has always been that way, the self-sacrificer." Eli closed the door behind him and shifted to a quieter, more conspiratorial tone. "That's how he died the first time, saving your Gran from Plumbers. But she caught him, pulled him back up, stopped his drain, you might say."

"And you?" Nara asked, realizing Eli telling this story, after all these years, meant that he knew all about this afterworld thing and knew that Nara knew now, too. How many people were in on this secret? "How did you meet Gran?"

"Carmen spun you an epic tale, didn't he? He's like that, will talk for days if you let him. I'm more direct. I was in a bad place, ready to throw my life away, powerless. Aizah pulled me back from the edge. We don't have time for lengthy narratives. The Plumbers are closing in. They known Aizah is here somewhere. She's been on their most wanted list for a while."

"And if they find her, they unplug her drain and she never wakes up."

"Got it in one."

"What can we do?"

"Generally, we run, or we hide, but neither of you is in any shape to run, and with your names in the computer systems, and on so many lips around here, hiding's not going to work either."

"So?"

"So, we fight."

"Fight death?"

"What better place to fight death than a hospital? They're more like death's minions, anyway, which are innumerable, incorporeal, and unkillable."

"Oh, so no worries," Nara snarked. "Will anything in the bag help? I was bringing Gran some stuff to help her if she woke up, but Carmen made me take a bunch of weird stuff from the Traitor's apartment."

"The Traitor... is... is here?" Eli's face grew stony. He caught himself, and his tone shifted from stuttering surprise to cold efficiency. "I'll survey the equipment you brought. Might need to lift some things from hospital supplies or other rooms. You just rest, focus on being still. Conserve your energy in case plan A fails and we really do need to run. I saw a wheelchair around the corner. Can't risk you learning crutches on the fly and with a broken wing, to boot."

"Run? But what about Gran? We can't just leave her."

"It's what she would want, for you to survive. She's had a long life. We've discussed this many times."

"You've talked about her being in a coma and having to run away?"

"We've discussed contingency plans to get you to safety if things went sideways, and she was incapacitated, unable to protect you herself as she has done all your life."

"If she had that power, why are my parents dead? My uncles?"

"That's not for me to say. They made their own choices."

"They chose to die? Nobody does that."

"Not usually without good reason. Our reasons for everything we do are our own. Now shush. I'm thinking." Eli bent over the bag, pulling out the brass bowl and setting it on Nara's bedside table. From it, he drew every bead, every leaf, every bone, observing, cataloging each in his mind and laying them out like an artist creating a palette from which to paint.

"I don't suppose you want to tell me what all these things are, what they're for?"

"No time now, maybe later. You'll need to learn it all at some point, but it'd be best if your Gran taught you. Like reasons, magic is very individual. Your body, your spirit, are part of what you're making, your instrument, if you will. How I see or use a particular herb or feather, or what have you, will be slightly different to how you will use it."

"Like words. We all kind of understand each other most of the time, but individual words like 'love' and 'blue' don't bring the exact same things to mind for each person."

"Exactly. Understanding that puts you a big step past most people already. Leave it to Aizah to teach you without letting you *know* she's teaching you... Mmm, I can tell Carmen chose these things, but I can also see her influence."

"What can you tell me about her?"

"I'm not talking about her right now. We need to focus."

"Yes, yes we do," a new voice, female, adult, broke into the conversation. Nara hadn't even heard the door open and close. The nurse, who had helped him back into bed, stood by the door. As he watched, her entire person blurred and re-solidified. A woman who looked like a younger version of Gran, but with lighter eyes and darker hair, stood, knees bent, arms slightly raised, as though she was about to leap across the room or tumble away. Her white uniform was replaced by a brown leather jacket over a blocky-print blouse and blue jeans.

"You have some balls showing up here now," Eli said, acid on his tongue. He stared at her for a moment, then turned back to the collection of oddments, "And using *their* disguise magic."

Their magic? Nara wondered. *The* Plumbers'?

"That's not fair. You know I've always wanted to come back, to be here for him. She kept me away."

"With good reason. You nearly killed her. Nearly killed us all," Eli spat.

"I... I thought I was doing the right thing."

"Everyone thinks they're doing the right thing. That doesn't *make* it right," Eli deflected her reasoning again.

"As to the illusion, magic is magic. You think some of what Aizah taught you didn't come from them? You can't fight them on your own."

"Not much choice. The boy's not remotely ready. I'm not going to let them take her without trying."

"You're not hearing me," the woman said, drawing a large pouch from the inner pocket of her jacket. The bag was royal blue leather, with a radiating dot pattern in rings of color painted onto one side.

"Oh, I *hear* you. I'm choosing not to let you 'fool me twice' as the saying goes," the man said.

"But you *are* being foolish. I can help you. Narito, tell him. Tell him you trust me."

"What? I don't know you. If you're the Traitor, the one who put my Gran in danger, I don't think I want to."

"You don't know me? How... What did she do?" The woman looked back and forth between Nara and Eli, finally settling on the latter. "Eli?" Her voice softened, the truth that Nara clearly hadn't put together yet hanging right over her, but she needed him to say it.

"What would you have done? Your daughter betrayed you... Tried to kill you... Left a bunch of other bodies to mourn and deal with, then vanished. Left with a child to raise, how do you explain things? How do you quiet the fires of betrayal and anger? Hatred, even? We figured the dull ache of a mother he couldn't quite remember was better than the weight of what you dumped on his shoulders. Son of a traitor to life itself. A traitor responsible for family members' deaths, his *father's* death. How would he ever stand straight under that burden? How would he ever become a man?"

"You had no right," the woman managed to choke out.

"You destroyed decades, *centuries* of work. We were doing something important, disrupting a system of oppression. And in the end, you were gone. A right? What we didn't have was a *choice*." Even numbed by drugs, confused by the words flying back and forth, Nara picked up an important piece of what they were putting down. *Daughter. Son.*

$$\{\ 16\ \}$$

"Mom?" The word slipped from his lips like his last breath, his heart feeling like it stopped in his chest. The revelation didn't bring the flood of memories he expected in retrospect. This was just another person, like billions of others he had never met roaming the Earth, and he knew the same amount about her as anyone he saw on TV or in a magazine. Less.

"Sí, Narito, and despite what some may think, I am here to help. I can't apologize for doing what I thought was right, though I will admit that I wasn't seeing the big picture. How could I? I was only thirty. You were three. In the grand scheme, were were both babies." Eli snorted at this, arranging objects on the tray over and over again, growing more agitated with the results.

"You have any damned indigo in there?" he asked finally, looking at the bag in the woman's hand.

"You know I don't. I was never a pigment worker. I was always music and whispers."

"Whispers... Learned from the Plumbers, no doubt."

"That doesn't make it bad. Some might say one's strongest weapon is understanding how one's enemy operates."

"Don't throw my words back at me. Not after all this."

"I heard what you said to Nara. I think you would be a fine teacher. Better than Mother in some ways." Eli snorted again.

"Flattery? Really? You think that's who I am, Isa?"

"Just honesty. You might follow Mother like she's the latest coming of Christ, but she's just a woman who found a shiny object in a deep, dark cave and held on for the ride. Anyone who held on long enough would have ended up in the same place."

"Bite your tongue," Eli snarled. "She is a great woman, with a noble goal."

"Nobility is questionable," Nara's mother said. "Like many endeavors, at its core, it's self-serving."

"You can just go away if you're not going to be of use," Eli said in that flat tone he used when he was truly angry. Nara had only heard it couple of times. He shivered.

"So... Mom... Mother? I don't even know what to call you... Where have you been?" The woman Eli had called "Isa" turned toward him. Her lips pressed together. Her eyebrows knit. She looked as though she might cry.

"My name is Isabella Leon Cordoba, but you used to call me 'Mama,' as I called Aizah when I was young." She took his free hand in both of hers as she spoke. Tears welled in her eyes. "But I suppose you don't remember that, or the house where we lived, in the hills above the city, or the lake where your father and I would take you those first few summers, to build sandcastles and teach you to swim."

"No, I- I don't remember any of that," Nara admitted. "But why? Why don't I remember?"

"Your grandmother apparently thought it best, rather than having difficult discussions with you about the way the larger world worked..." Eli cleared his throat, interrupting Isa. "Doing what she thought was best... for you... or for herself..." Eli grabbed the leather bag violently from the table and started removing items. Many were the same as the ones he already had. The stash Carmen had made was from Nara's mother's set up, after all.

"Simeon was gone, and Talia, Elsbeth, Giovanni, Li Zhang... the Plumbers did a real number on the group that day," Eli rebutted.

"It's a cult. You can say the word, an immortality *cult.*"

"Cults follow charismatic swindlers. Aizah may be persuasive, but she's no charlatan. I wouldn't be staring at my two hundred thirties this summer if she was."

"Every cult leader has some little trick, some cheat to convince the rubes," Isa said.

"Remind me why you're here again? What is your purpose? Are you just here as a distraction while your Plumber buddies nail down our location and set up a floodgate?"

"They're not my buddies. I'm on their list now, too. I have my own reasons for working against them."

"Raul?" Eli asked, a sneer sneaking across his face. Isa flinched. It was a cruel strike, but Nara didn't know how.

"...yes," Isa accepted in a small voice. "The promise of eternity loses its luster when you've lost your reasons for wanting to live in the first place."

"A child's point of view. You said before you were just a baby when this all happened. That's your only excuse, but it sounds like you're still hanging onto it."

"Do I still love Raul? Have I missed him and Nara every day since we were parted? Yes. If that's 'childish' in your eternal wisdom, then so be it, but it's mine. It's how *I* feel, not how someone trained me, or directed me or forced me to be."

"No one was forcing you to do or be anything," Eli said. The lights flickered again. "Here we go. I wish I'd known to bring my mojo bag. We'd have a fight to bring them. As it is, we're just going to get flushed like goldfish."

"Let me look at that," Isa said, backing away from Nara and turning toward the table. "This is all perfectly good material. I don't know why you're so bull-headed. You just have to..." she said, waving her hands and mumbling something Nara couldn't quite process. He could hear the sounds, but they didn't always seem to correspond with the movements of her mouth.

After a few seconds, some of the bones rattled on the table, the feathers spinning up into the air in controlled arcs. "Methos," she said a few times, nodding her head toward one end of the table. Finally, Eli caught on or accepted that he was aiding her instead of the other way around and picked up and opened a stout glass jar resembling an ink bottle. He didn't need to pour, though, as a stream of brownish liquid rose into the air like a serpent from a basket.

"What in the name of Pete is going on in here?" demanded a new voice from the door. A nurse stood, aghast at the flurry of detritus spinning over the rolling table. "Patients have to eat off that!"

"We're sorry, ma'am. This is really very important," Nara said.

"I don't care how important you think it is, she better stop it right now or I'm calling security." Isa grunted with effort as the materials suddenly slammed together in what Nara expected to be a violent explosion or crash but instead resulted in a disk the size of a saucer with bones and feathers and wood and leather fused into overlapping spirals. "Great. Arts and crafts hour is over, now get out," the newcomer said. The lights flickered again. "Is that you? Did you do that? Disturbing the electrons or what have you?"

"No, it's them. They're coming. We need to get to Aizah," Isa said, half to the nurse and half to Eli and Nara.

"I'll get the wheelchair," Eli said, all business now, emotion vanished from his tone.

"You will not! Those are for hospital use only! By qualified personnel!" The nurse continued, trying to block Eli's exit, but he simply passed right through her. She screamed and fainted, crumpling to the linoleum like a dropped sheet.

"Smart, great," Isa said, "now we have to move her." She left the device she had made on the table and began to do just that, grabbing the larger woman by her wrists and dragging her into the room. As she cleared the doorway, Eli returned with the wheelchair, rolling it to the side of the bed and assisting Nara into it.

"I'm not saying I don't want to go, but what good am I in this equation? I don't know any magic unless the severed thumb trick or pulling quarters out of ears counts," Nara said.

"We need to be all together. Even if you can't wield the power, you can... be a source."

"A battery, just half a step above stay-in-the-van guy. Great." Nara gave a sarcastic laugh.

"It's a way for you to help. More than she could offer," Eli said, indicating the nurse.

"You didn't... she'll be all right... right?"

"Of course. I just disrupted her energies a bit when I passed through her," Eli explained as he pushed Nara toward the elevator. "She gave me the idea herself. Don't give me that look. She'll wake up with a headache, a little vertigo. A good night's sleep will see her right as rain."

"Rain..." Nara repeated as the notion sparked a memory of the place he'd been seeing in his dreams. Carmen had said the rain was the spirits of the living from this world, seeding life in the next, but the rain had eaten the window glass, made the door less real... There was something there, but he couldn't put his finger on it.

"Nara!" Still another new voice called out. No, now new... familiar... Nara looked around, and saw Matty coming from the next room. She had a few bandages on her forehead and arms but looked more or less intact. As she passed the doorway to stand over him, he saw Rodolpho, arm in a sling like his own, and a lot more bandages around his head, chest, elsewhere, monitors like Gran's standing watch over him, beeping and showing jagged lines. "How are you? They didn't tell us you were right next door, or I would have come visited."

"How is Rodolpho?"

"Pretty banged, up, but Carmen saved us... Is he in the room on the other side?"

"He didn't make it. I think he went down the crevice into the sewers, or maybe he got sucked up with the building after all..."

"Oh, I'm so sorr-" Matty began, but then Eli started pushing Nara toward the elevator again.

"Sorry, I guess I have to go. I'll check in later," Nara said as Matty stood by Rodolpho's door.

"What was all that about?" Eli asked.

"Wasn't that the lady from the news?"

"Yeah, it's a long story," Nara said.

{ 17 }

The lights flickered again as they went up in the elevator. A red light shone from the panel with the floor buttons, but then the big metal box jerked and began to rise again. Nara forced out a breath and released his death-grip on the wheelchair's arm. Isa moved one hand from holding Gran's tote against her body to squeeze his shoulder. He couldn't bring himself to look up at her. He immediately felt terrible. His stomach churned.

The moment they rolled out of the elevator, the lights flickered rapidly before the whole place went dark. Emergency lights flashed above a few doorways. High-pitched tones screamed into the main space from the rooms along the periphery.

"Four thirteen," Nara said, pointing in the direction of Aizah's room.

"I can feel her," Eli said.

"So that means she's still here, right? They didn't... flush her yet."

"You'd know. We'd all feel it, for one," Eli said.

"And the building would probably implode for two. The Plumbers won't be taking any chances this time. This is their moment to remove a very old, very irritating thorn from their side," Isa said.

"Less commentary, more spellweaving. You have the thing you made?"

"I call it a corusca, yes," Isa replied.

"Good, we're about to need it." The sirens and warnings, visible and audible, all ceased at once. Thick shadows raced across the linoleum, splashing up over desks and counters like the sea against rocks, blotting out everything.

"I know this isn't really the time, but if this is all about energies and experience filling us up and flowing out of us like water... what is with all the shadow and darkness?" Nara asked.

"That's actually a great question, mijo," Isa said. "It has to do with the relative energy levels. By and large, we live at a higher energy level, which is why salmon, what we call those who manage to return from the next world, are wispy and insubstantial, and why we're so powerful down there."

"School later. Right now, we need to survive the day," Eli said, plowing Nara through the drifting shadows. He opened Aizah's door and dragged Nara backward through it. Isa followed them in and closed the door. She wedged a chair under the handle like in the movies, then backed up to stand in the middle of the open area. Gran's bag at her feet, she lifted the corusca and began rotating her hands above and below it while it hovered between, spinning. It twirled faster and faster until a pale blue light burst from its edge, forming a dome. She then pulled the above hand in and changed the pattern of movement.

***

When Nara's eyes recovered, he stood in the wreckage of the farmhouse. The roof had collapsed, and something was nesting in the angle the decaying beam and shingles made with the wall. The chimney slumped, a jagged stump above the hearth. Rain beat down on the dwindling remains of the furniture and firewood stack, pooling in places on the warped floor.

"Wow... What happened here?"

"H-hello?" The voice sounded tired and far away. The straw, gathered under the broken roof, shifted and a small face appeared. Nara walked toward her, then as he recognized her dress and general form, began to run. It took what seemed like minutes to get to her. "You're that little boy!"

"You're that big girl... Or you were... what happened?"

"The rain never stops. It just washes everything away into the sea. I guess I just wasn't strong enough to keep it back, to hold my place here. I only *thought* I was a giant. This place is all about experiences and will, you know, 'you gotta want it.' Oh, did I want it, and it was magnificent, for a long while... Well, a long while for a person, I suppose, not so long in the life of the universe. It's almost over now."

"What is?"

"My life, my dream, my connection to..." she fell quiet and simply pointed toward the clouds.

"Life... do you... know where you are?" Nara asked as gently as he could. This was the afterlife, he was sure of it now, the rain, the strange constructs which had somehow congealed from the ideas and experiences of all those who passed, falling down on the next world. The girl nodded.

"I know. There are other worlds, up and down, different energy levels, like electrons in their shells," she said. The words seemed odd coming from such a young person. What could she know of electron shells? He'd only learned about them in high school. But then, her speech patterns, the sophistication of her ideas... Perhaps not everything was what it looked like here, even more than back home.

"If you don't mind me asking... how old were you when you... uh, when you came here?"

"The first time? Oh, my thirties, kicked in the head by a donkey. But I found something when I got down here, something that buoyed me up, pulled me back. It was something inextricably bound to the world I was used to, the 'living' world they call it, as if it's the only one. This world has life a plenty, and worlds above brim with so much energy they can do big magic, transforming into animals and building castles in a day."

"I saw what seemed to be pretty big magic in my world, a whole building consumed by shadow and sucked down here, my uncle transformed into some kind of long-fingered monstrosity..."

"Uncle?" The girl said, head tilting to one side.

"Carmen. He's not really my uncle by blood, I don't think. Who knows anything anymore? I just found out my mother's still alive after thinking she'd died at the same time as my dad when I was little."

"Carmen? Not a baker, a donut maker?"

"How did you know that?" Nara asked, backing away slowly and talking even slower.

"You don't recognize me? I suppose I didn't recognize you, either, Narito," the girl said, gradually seeming much older. For a moment, she looked like the mother he'd just met, then her hair grayed and skin wrinkled.

"Gran? What? But you're in a coma."

"That's pretty close to dead. It lets the spirit wander. I came back to this farm I'd built ages ago. I was surprised it was still here, but I supposed it had always lurked in the back of my mind, a pleasant memory. The amount of energy it would take to maintain from up there is practically nothing. But if I'm in a coma, my connection to that world, that power, is fading. Do you know what happened? Am I finally dying?"

"Eli seems to think so. The Plumbers are in the hospital. The whole floor went dark. They already took a building where Carmen lived. I barely escaped with the reporter and her cameraman."

"I don't know what that means. I wish I had time to hear the whole story, but this..." she held up a knobby, wrinkled hand, "Means I'm about at the end of my rope."

"Don't say that. You're all I have."

"I know you think that, but you've got friends, Eli, and it sounds like your mother has finally showed herself, for what that's worth..."

"I don't really know what happened with her, but she's with Eli now, trying to fend off the Plumbers. I think she's..."

"Plumbers, eh? What do you know about *them*? Mm?"

"Nothing really, just that they're called that because they go around unplugging drains, letting people's spirits flow through to the next world when they're stuck, or have stuck themselves... in the world we know."

"Mm, decent assessment, as far as it goes. It's the natural cycle, the circle of life as the song says. Things die so other things can eat them and all that. The body feeds physical beings in the world above as the spirit nourishes those below."

"Sure, that's fine for rabbits and wolves, but we're people. If there's one thing we do, it's buck the natural trend. Vaccines, domestication of animals and plants, clothing, houses, cars, planes, wholesale genetic engineering... We've always mastered nature, bent it to our will," Nara said.

"And how has that worked for the world above?" Gran asked shrewdly, squinting and giving him a wry smile. "Pollution, extinctions, war... I've been at this for a while, and sometimes, yeah, there's no difference between a dog and a man, or a whale, or a tree. They all die. It's just that this world is fed by the energy that fills humanity over its lifetime," she finished, pointing upward.

"So the Plumbers... they're sent by Death, or God or something?" Nara asked. Gran shrugged. "What are you?" Nara asked, not sure if he really wanted an answer.

"I am a woman who decided the natural order wasn't good enough. I suppose you could say I was a rebel. But maybe my fight is over now. Without the tear, we're just another couple of raindrops."

"The tear?"

"It was a tool, an anchor, kind of, that would always bring one back to the world above when one was drained. It would attach itself to one's essence, the memories, the *soul*, and allow one to travel back and forth without being spread out, subverting nature."

"What did this 'tear' look like?" Nara asked, certain that he knew already.

"It hardly matters now. There's no time for an epic journey to recover it. I'll be dead by morning. They'll have won, and things will go back to normal."

"Indulge your grandson one last time," Nara prodded. Gran heaved a sigh.

"It's teardrop-shaped, about yay big," Gran spread her first finger and thumb, "made of cobalt crystal and..." Nara produced something from his pocket and held it in his palm.

"Carmen called it a gota. I thought it was because of the shape, but I think it's been pulling me back and forth between the worlds all day, a raindrop caught in a storm."

"Where did you get it?" Gran asked, reaching out a brown hand to take it from him.

{ **18** }

"Not so fast, '*Aizah!*'" A voice boomed. The broken roof rose up and tipped away, sliding down outside the house with a crash. Nara pulled his hand back to him, still gripping the bauble. In the corner of the farmhouse stood the girl he had seen before, full size and practically glowing with energy.

"Give it to me!" The woman closer to him screamed as he had never heard her do in life.

"The truth is there's no real reason to die," the giant girl said, "The whole thing's a scam. If you're smart enough, strong enough, you can, as you say, plug your drain, prevent yourself from being emptied, lost in the tides of this place." The woman he had thought was Gran twisted and writhed, spewing black fog, which spun into a new form: a hooded figure with a scythe in two skeletal hands, matching the girl's size. "Nice, Plumber, very dramatic, you're the 'arbiters of life and death, right hand to the final judge' blah blah." The girl ducked under a scythe swipe and launched herself off the crumbling chimney, sending gray stone tumbling out of the house while she flew across to the robed figure, slamming it into the opposite wall.

"Stop your slander!" The Plumber shrieked, upright again.

"You just want beasts easily led to the slaughter so your kind can reap the benefits! Eh? *Reap*?" the young, giant version of Gran said. "What's good for the goose has no place in my life. I don't want to eat bugs and pond weeds or chew my cud all day. There's too much life to live in the tiny slice of time you arbitrarily allot us!"

"We are the designated marshals of Death itself!" The creature leapt toward Gran, curved blade aimed right at her heart. She threw her hands up, creating a hemispherical shield that flashed as the weapon was deflected, sending the Plumber tumbling away. "Regulators of a system that has been in place for eons!"

"Just because someone takes a name and gets people to follow them doesn't mean they're what they say they are. I was always straightforward with my people. I told them what I wanted to achieve, what I know we can achieve as a people, but I never claimed to be anything I wasn't. Unlike your lot!"

"You are an aberration! A flaw in the system!" The Plumber rose, discarding the wood-handled scythe, new blades curving out from the sleeves of its robes.

"I am a woman who saw an unfair system that separated families, loved ones, tribes, and nations and decided it needed changing. I suppose you could say I was a rebel. But how often is the oppressive regime right?"

"There are always malcontents. No one wants to bear the burden of responsibility."

"Run, Narito! Get the gota to me in the living world!" the giant child said. He looked between the black robed figure and the giant who spoke like his Gran.

"I don't know how to make it work, it just always did its thing on its own."

"You must learn to master it," Gran said as the creature howled at the sky. Other howls returned from the clouds, followed by black specks, too many black specks, which grew quickly as they converged on the farm. "Or at least take the first step toward mastery. Now go!"

Nara ran out the front door and across the yard. He felt exposed, a sitting duck for an army of creatures plummeting from the clouds. Surely they saw him.

With a laugh, Gran punched a section of wall, shattering the boards. Hundreds of splinters flew out and landed in the grass. In seconds, each one grew up into a clone of Nara, dressed as he often did in white t-shirt and black vest, jeans, and sneakers. They each looked around for a fraction of a second, chose a direction, and ran. Realizing he would want to blend in, he ran too, taking a slightly different angle to where he had been going before, to make things tougher for any Plumber who wanted to pull his plug.

"Come on, gota, any time now. I'd like to go back and see Gran in the hospital. I realize it's probably loco up there right now, with Mama and Eli fighting the Plumbers..." He looked up and wondered just how many of these things were there. Were they like grim reapers from the movies? Present at every death? Somehow that didn't really make sense to him. It was probably just one of those Hollywood things. Whatever works for the excitement factor. Still, there were a lot. The creatures swooped down in waves like a murmuration of birds. They grabbed up many of his clones and carried them away, abductors and abductees alike screaming.

"Go, gota!" He tried to say it forcefully without yelling so loudly as to draw attention to himself. A second later, he heard one of his clones yell, "Gota, go!" Other variations spread across the island that, once massive, seemed nowhere near large enough now.

Plowing through the tall grass, he came abruptly to the sea, lapping around the roots of the grass. One of his clones splashed into the water with a surprised shriek a dozen feet to his left. As he watched that one thrash in the water, the surging sea tore handfuls of green stalks away. Some floated off, some sank into the unnaturally blue water. The clone reverted to a splinter and drifted away. "Now what?" he asked himself. "Gran made the farmhouse. Can't you make a little boat?"

He held the gota out, gripped in his fist, which he aimed straight on, then palm down at the water, trying to will a boat into being. But he couldn't figure out what it should look like. He had a feeling a clear picture in his head was what he needed. But what boat did he know? Huck Finn's raft? Simple, but it didn't seem like it would fare very well on the waves he saw out there. The Love Boat from the show Gran watched all the time? Too big. How would he make the whole thing in time? Or steer it? He just didn't know enough about boats.

Wait, no, a pirate ship. Big enough to sail the seas of the afterlife, but not too unwieldy. He could envision a small crew, who could handle the sails and such. Yes, a pirate ship with great rectangular sails and two, no, three masts... As the details fleshed themselves out in his mind, a dark mass rose up from the water, forming a wood-hulled boat with three square sails. A pirate flag flapped above a crow's nest on the main mast. A slew of folk in red and white striped shirts or modified naval coats hustled around the decks.

"Ahoy, Captain, ready to board?" one of the sailors asked, waving others over to lower the gangplank to the grassy brink.

"Aye, let us flee this isle for fairer lands!" Nara called back. At the top of the ramp, one of the sailors slapped a hat upon his head while another slung a coat over his shoulders.

"What course, Captain?" The first sailor asked him, bowing and extending a spyglass. Nara took the device and ran up the stairs to the wheel. He peered out across the churning sea, searching for any sign. Uncountable odd sights met him through the glass, but not a one whispered to him a destination. The only place he wanted to be was back in the world he knew, beside his Mama and Eli.

Back at Gran's island, he saw an old school biplane sputter into the sky. A moment later, a rocket shot up, trailing sparkling white exhaust. Another fled on a griffon. There was a jet ski, a hot air balloon, a massive paper airplane, thin blue lines of a sheet of notebook paper evident, angled this way and that. Cadres of Plumbers chased each one. Some descended upon his ship.

"Sail Ho! The black flag flies!" a tall, thin pirate cried, pointing into the sky. "Man the guns!"

"Skinny Slim!" Nara said, naming the man on the fly, "You're my first mate. You have the helm for evasive maneuvers. I'll see what I can come up with for more... modern defenses."

"Yes sir!" Skinny snapped a sharp salute and ran up a set of stairs to the deck, where the wheel stood. Plumbers swept toward the ship from different directions. Nara felt a weight on his hip and looked down to find a flintlock pistol hanging in a holster. He drew it, marveling at the heavy barrel and ancient styling. He pointed it at one of the clusters of fluttering black robes and pulled the trigger. The hammer slammed forward, creating a spark. The weapon bucked in his hand, sending its muzzle skyward. The Plumbers shifted their paths, like a school of fish swimming around an obstacle, and angled toward him. Nara pulled the trigger again, but nothing happened.

"Gotta reload, Captain!" a nearby sailor said, hauling a cannon around to take his own shot.

"Reload?" he muttered to himself, "How the Hell do I do that?" Shaking his head, he tried to picture something more modern, as he'd promised, but the only image he could summon was the old plastic laser gun from Carmen's old video game console. All around him, cannons exploded. Plumbers dodged and scattered, but a couple of them were thrust away at such speeds that Nara thought they'd been obliterated, until he saw their forms fading into the distance. "Nice one, gentlemen! Reload for another volley!" The first part of his address brought up a wave of laughter, but the men and women knew their business and were soon ramming new shot home and taking aim on the reforming flight of Plumbers.

Nara aimed the plastic gun at the Plumbers and squeezed the trigger. A brilliant green beam leapt forth, cutting through one of the black-clad forms, which then fell with a splash into the sea. Heartened, he fired again and again, with varying degrees of success. He had never been terribly good at video games, and never held a real gun, but as the Plumbers assaulting them thinned, he watched torrents of red and blue beams light up other areas of the sky and hoped his clones were taking out their fair share as well.

When the last Plumber that seemed interested in the pirate ship fell, and the air was heady with black powder smoke, Nara turned back to the idea of finding cover, perhaps a hidden cove behind a curtain of stone and thick trees, where he could think, rest, and experiment with the gota. Panning back across the horizon, he spotted just the place, a mountain whose feet dipped into the sea and whose head was wreathed in clouds. Perhaps he could even walk back home...

"That way, but you know... sneaky-like. The... King's men are after us, and we need to find a quiet berth where we can catch our breath." He stuffed the glass in his pocket and took the wheel, spinning it one way while his first mate called out orders regarding the sails to the crew. He banked this way and that, finally describing a roundabout course to the island he had spotted. When it was visible to the naked eye, he pointed. "There we are," Nara said. "Can you thread us in between the cliffs around the left... erm... port side and drop anchor in the cove beyond, Skinny Slim?" He asked his first mate.

"'Course, Captain sir. Will you be below, in your quarters, then?" He hadn't even considered having his own luxurious pirate captain cabin, with a large wooden globe and massive desk at one end...

"That I shall," Nara said. "That I shall. Thank you, Skinny."

"My pleasure, as ever Captain," the first mate said, taking the wheel and yelling out orders to the crew again.

The Captain's quarters were sumptuous, with thick, overlapping rugs covering much of the floor, a large, soft bed framed in by red velvet curtains hanging from four dark wood posts, and a wall of books, maps, and bottles with bars to keep them on their shelves. The massive desk was larger than his bed back home. At the end, a rack held half a dozen swords of varying design and decoration. The back wall of the room was a broad, many-paned window, through which he could see a storm of black rain falling upon what he knew must be Gran's island. How would he help her? How would he get back?

"That is an interesting question," a vaguely familiar voice said with excessive sibilance.

"What?" Nara asked, turning to see the enormous snake with rainbow scales and flicking gray tongue, coiled up, taking up a third of the room. Even as vast as it was, it was smaller than before.

"Well, one has to fit one's surroundings. One cannot simply appear as a snake head. It doesn't have the same impact."

"Sure, sure, I can see that," Nara said. Despite the fact that his visitor was a giant predator, that would strike fear into most people at a fraction of the size, he felt almost at ease with the creature. Was it because he had seen it in a dream?

"Is it not the dream of each of us to be dreamed of by a prince?" the serpent said, apparently able to hear his thoughts.

"A prince?"

"Of course, grandson of a queen. What else does that make you? I'm not very much up on the hierarchy. We don't have such things down here, except in places, of course, where we do. So much filters down, and you all hold onto the strangest things. Why should one person be so much more important than all of the others?"

"I don't know about any of that either. I just need to get back up there."

"You went before, just flew up into the clouds. I didn't think to see you again so soon. Though, again, one's sense of time isn't always the keenest. It doesn't always move at the same rate as itself, and if it can't be bothered to agree with itself, why should I?"

"A point, I suppose, but still, my Gran..."

"I understand incompletely." The serpent nodded.

"Don't you mean 'completely?'"

"No, it never does to be completely certain. Just ask Heisenberg. Or was it Schrödinger?"

"Huh?"

"Don't worry on it... So, *Captain*, what are we onto now? What is your plan?"

"A whole swarm of Plumbers is attacking Gran, down here and up there at the same time. I have no idea how to save her."

"Don't you?" The serpent flashed a deep blue, reminding him of something. He reached into his pocket.

"The gota?"

"If that's what you call it. It is a legendary device in this place. There are precious few ways to go 'upstream,' as the salmon call it. They're so eager to thrust themselves up and up, forgetting that creature they've named themselves for arrives at his destination -when he arrives- and promptly dies from exhaustion."

"But if one is already dead, what can really happen? They can't die again..."

"Yes and no... These beings have already overcome the odds, remembering themselves, remaining whole enough to be coherent creatures, instead of being turned into compost fertilizer and cast into the field to feed the crops. But in burning all of that energy, they lose that cohesion, they fade and fall apart."

"You seem pretty coherent."

"Thank you." The great head tilted a few degrees to the right.

"What I mean is, were you born here? Or are you from up there? Were you a person before you were a... giant rainbow snake?"

"Everything you see here, with rare exception, was born here, except the keepers, the Plumbers, as you call them."

"And where are they from?"

"I couldn't say."

"Couldn't? Or wouldn't?" The serpent brought its head back, coils moving forward to either side of its great face. It seemed to Nara like it was a shrug.

"Do you know how to use it? The gota? Can you help me figure it out?" Nara held up the blue glass, impregnated with so many colors and shapes, peering at it in the light from over his shoulder. The colors flashed and glittered as though they were their own rainbow, caught inside a raindrop the size of his thumb.

"You seem to have a decent hold on it. You just made all this." The serpent peered around as Nara spun the globe.

"But I need to know how it gets me back 'upstream.'"

"At the risk of repeating myself, 'You just made all this.'"

"So I should just... stay in the afterworld? Forget about Gran and all she's done for me? Let the Plumbers have her? Pull her plug..." Nara was having an idea, but it formed slowly... "Is there a way to know where she'll come down? Can one collect all of someone as they come down from the clouds?"

"You want to wait until she's done and save her on this side?"

"It's stupid, isn't it?" Nara's shoulders slumped. He leaned back against the desk.

"It seems a difficult and complicated way to accomplish the goal. Which isn't to say it can't be done by someone with the will..."

"I need more than will. I need knowledge. How would I collect the drops? How would I get just hers? All of hers? It wouldn't do us much good to get half of her... or a tenth..."

"What are your thoughts?" the serpent asked.

"Don't you know? You were answering them before I began speaking aloud," Nara said with a hint of accusation. He couldn't tell if the creature really wanted to help him, or was just amusing itself at his expense. "Gran would know how to teach me. She's an expert if there ever was one. She's been doing this, going back and forth, for decades, centuries... longer? I don't even know. We talk all the time. I thought we knew everything about each other, but this... it's literally a whole world of secrets."

"So you want to talk to her, to... find out how to get to her? How does that work?"

"She's here, a part of her. I ran before. She told me to, and she was right, but this..." He held up the gota again. "If I can learn to use it, go save her, the part of her that's here, from the Plumbers, she can tell me how to get back up to her, how to really save her."

"That sounds like *a* plan... or at least a '*pla*.' How will you implement it?"

"You said that time works differently here... How much time do I have to train?" Nara asked, thinking of the great movies with training montages, main characters running up stairs and punching sides of beef, tumbling and leaping and, finally, strapping on boots and bandoleers of weapons.

"I really couldn't say..." The serpent writhed as though uncomfortable answering the question. Or perhaps, Nara thought, uncomfortable lying. Serpents were associated with deceit going back to the Abrahamic Bible, back to the stories from where that collection of works had descended...

"Then I better get to it," Nara said.

Leaving Skinny Slim in charge of the ship, he stood on the crescent of sandy beach at the base of the green foothills of the great mountain.

"What will I need to do this?" he wondered to himself, "Flying would be awesome, weapons, armor maybe, or a way to grab her and pull her from the fight, assuming she's still there fighting... Maybe rescuing her from a jail of some sort? Do they have jails here?"

"They have everything here, everything you bring with you from above, or can make from the fragments..." the rainbow serpent said, full size again and coiled upon a nearby hill. "Simpler is usually better, though. Doesn't do to have too many moving parts, too much complexity." Nara was reminded of the farmhouse, falling apart and even the materials fading from fully-realized textures and shapes to simplified blocks. The fire was the first to go...

"Something simple." Nara nodded, focusing on the sandy patch before him. He swept his hands up dramatically, firstly to one side, then the other. Not a grain budged. He deepened his stance, like a martial artist preparing to break boards. He then took a deep breath and forced it out while pushing his hands forward. Nothing. He dropped his hands, letting out a sigh of frustration and defeat.

The sand spun up in a small dust devil, then dropped back to the beach. He glanced over at the serpent, but it appeared to be asleep, its head tucked into its coils. "Some moral support..."

He tried again, recreating the movements he'd made as best he could. A handful of sand rose up and flopped over like a wavelet approaching shore, becoming indiscernible amongst millions of other grains. "Focus," he chided himself. "You've got this. It's in your blood. Gran made a whole farm, buildings, stone walls, a garden. You made a ship. Why are you having trouble now?"

"That is a question. Perhaps it is a matter of... motivation..." The rainbow serpent uncoiled from his hilltop and encircled Nara, giving him the sensation of standing on a train platform, the cars barreling by. The multi-colored head swayed above him, then dove.

Remembering Eli walking through the nurse, Nara gripped the gota in his fist and tumbled forward into the serpent's iridescent body. Squeezing his eyes tight, he pictured himself rolling out the other side of the coils onto the sand. Instead, he slammed headfirst into the slick scales and fell over onto his side as a maw, with fangs the length of his arm, plunged toward him.

{ 20 }

Eyes clamped shut again, limbs pulled into a fetal position, Nara braced for consumption. What he felt was an electric hum racing across his... what even was he? Was this his body? Or his spirit? His consciousness at the very least, he thought.

"This is not the time for philosophy," the rainbow serpent said as it pulled back.

"Maybe... maybe not," Nara replied. "It's certainly not a matter of simply leaping... Unless it is..." If everything here was derived from human experience, it would make sense for human experience to see him through. He needed to go up, and the mountain, as he had noted earlier, would get him pretty close, if not all the way to the roof of clouds topping this world. The serpent uncoiled from around him, eager to see his thought play out. Nara ran.

Emerald draped foothills rose into gray cliffs topped by jungle. From the rich forest rose ridges, which converged somewhere above the cloud line. At least, Nara hoped they did. He heard the rasp of scales and hiss of breath behind him as the rainbow serpent followed him up the first hill, then the next and the next, into the forest, where the trees were often so close together that the giant creature slammed into trunks to get through.

"Yes! Don't slow now! Go! Go!" The serpent urged him on. Despite the attempt to bite him earlier, Nara felt the creature was on his side. Now, he ran up a narrow ridge of gray stone, the ground dropping away for hundreds of feet on either side. As he rose, the clouds grew closer. He braced himself for the rush of memories that had assaulted him when it rained.

Mist whirled around, chill to the touch, peppering him with tiny fragments of sensation. Each impulse was so small, so quick, it wasn't intrusive in itself, but added to what almost felt like... music. This wasn't overwhelming, but exhilarating. As Nara pushed on, up the slope, the wind grew more insistent, the ground colder, accumulating a sheen, then a thicker coating, of snow. He summoned a thick winter coat, with a fur lining around the hood, like he had seen in movies, but the growing cold only slapped his face and hands. He created a scarf, gloves, and heavier boots with good treads.

Visibility faded amid thick mist and heavier swirls of snow, but the shadow of the hidden peak solidified, showing him his goal. Nara pushed forward, buffeted, his footing dubious as the snow slid away. A distant screech stood out from the howling wind. He looked around, but saw nothing. Another came, impossible to place, but piercing, sending a different kind of shiver through him.

"Nara! Look out!" He thought he heard a voice in the distance, and a second shadow, wedge-shaped like the one before him, but on its side, appeared, growing larger, darker, and more distinct by the moment. He searched for a place to hide, a cave, or a rock, but there was nothing but whipping snow and the path forward and upward.

The second shadow shattered, becoming a swarm of dark forms speeding toward him. He ran harder, pushing himself as fast as he'd ever run, faster up the slope, through the snow into the wind. He felt as though his feet were blocks of ice, sliding over the ice, getting him nowhere. The tip of the shadow mountain to his side broke off and launched toward him, separating from the swarm. As it neared, it tore the air with scythe-like forelimbs, reaching for him. Nara ducked, dodging to the side. As he recovered and righted himself, his feet continued to slide. Eyes wide, he leaned forward, trying to make his feet move faster, finally throwing himself down in the snow, trying to spread out, to find any handhold, or at least increase his surface area to keep from sliding over the cliff.

"Help!" he cried out, "Gran! Carmen! Anyone!" Something gripped his wrist, pulling him up a few inches, but then he slipped through the hold, fingers forcing their way through his hand like he was made of jelly.

"Use the gota!" A voice whispered past the wind, penetrating the noise. "I can't help you like this. Too much of me is... out there somewhere," the other explained. Nara's hand went to his pocket. He grabbed the teardrop and the hand held him tight. He stopped sliding back and began creeping forward. "This isn't easy. You've gotten so big! Focus, mijo!"

Mijo? Nara thought, concentration faltering. He slipped closer to the rounded edge of the cliff, not a handhold in sight under the sliding snow. He peered through the sky borne snow but couldn't make out the face.

"I knew she would lead you to a bad end!" the other yelled into the wind, more forceful than before. Nara could feel the hand solidifying on his wrist as he spoke. "You shouldn't be here, not for a good..." the other pulled mightily, hauling Nara up the slope, "long..." another heave, "time!" A third, and Nara was back on the path. He pushed himself up to his feet.

"Papa?" he asked as he squinted at the other. He was younger than the youth remembered, if it was him at all. But why would a Plumber pretend to be his papa *and* save Nara?

"It's me, Narito. It's been so long, not that one has much of a sense of time in this place... But you're so big, almost grown. You're here because of Aizah." Nara nodded.

"Kind of. There are..." He struggled for the right word. Were the Plumbers people? Angels? Ghosts? "Beings after her. She's in the hospital."

"And your mother's there. I can feel her energy on you, and, last I knew, she had the gota," Papa explained.

"Yes, she gave it to me. I didn't know it at first, or recognize her... but that's not important. It's wonderful to see you!"

"You, too, mijo, but this not a good time for a reunion. We've got to get you out of here. Use the gota. Go back up. It's not your time."

"It wasn't your time when you came here, either."

"We all make choices. Mine led me here…" Nara reached out his free hand to caress his father's cheek. A shriek went up, multiplying quickly into a chorus bearing down on them. "Go!"

"But I just found you!" A wall of dark shapes advanced to Nara's right, curving around behind his father, hemming them in. He turned to his left to see a flood of sharp shadows flowing from that side as well. They were keeping their distance, at least until enough of them where here to ensure victory. Had they left Gran to chase him? Was she still alive? "Papa!" he cried out, feeling the same pull as he'd felt before, right from his center, backward up into the mist. He reached for the revenant.

"You'll see me again! Go help your mama and Aizah."

Gran! The spirals of Plumbers tightened, reaching upward, forming a cone like an upside down tornado, narrow tail whipping so close he could see individual faces, raking sickles at the end of each arm. He could feel himself being dragged up, faster and faster, but the Plumbers raced after him, closing the distance. The nearest swiped at him as the tip of the cone rose around him. A dozen Plumbers turned their scythes inward, forming a great maw that closed around him.

{ **21** }

Nara awoke, screaming, in the wheelchair in Gran's hospital room. At least, that's where he guessed he was. Gran's bed and monitors stood at the center of the space, Eli and Mama to either side swinging their arms and chanting spells. The corusca Mama had made spun above, creating an azure dome of light, like a new sky encapsulating them all. Outside the sky, nothing but darkness with foreboding metallic flashes that swirled in dizzying eddies.

"Don't look right at them. Don't let them into your head!" Mama warned.

"Welcome back, Nara," Eli said.

"Uh, hi guys…" he responded weakly, standing from his chair on unsteady feet. He shuffled forward, putting a hand on the footboard of Gran's bed for support. Nara looked down at the woman of untold mystery and boundless love, taking her hand in his, pressing the gota between them. "Come on, Gran. Come back to us. Regresa a *mí*."

"The teardrop!" something screeched from outside the dome. A rattle like hail followed, sparking flashes becoming a stream of flickering yellow and orange light. Dark streaks appeared in the blue light of the corusca's shield.

"You did it now, kiddo!" Eli said, grunting under the effort of sending his own attacks, "V"s of gold and green light, blazing arrowheads, through the breeches to strike the attackers in likewise accelerated volleys. "They really want that thing!"

Mama gasped, her chanted spell faltering waves of darkness, that rolled across the glowing field, revealing a wall of Plumbers circling like ebon sharks, reminding him of his escape from the afterworld atop the snowy peak. He pulled the gota away from Gran's hand and held it against her shoulder. The tension there fell away as the dome grew instantly brighter, forcing him to close his eyes. A fraction of a second later, something tore at his own shoulder. "Down! I got him!" Eli cried.

A "V" shot whizzed by Nara, singeing Mama's hair and ricocheting off the dome before striking the intruding Plumber, now a "Y" of black robes, with arms ending in curved sickle blades aimed at Mama. "No!" Nara yelled, a video game laser pistol forming in the hand of his cast-bound arm. There was no way he could aim like this.

The Plumber swooped in. Nara pulled Mama aside, thrusting his cast in to block the blades. They bit into the plaster, dislodging chunks. A barrage of gold and green chevrons struck it in a line from one shoulder diagonally across what passed for a chest, severing its form. It fell back, the blades caught in the cast the last to fade into spinning black sparks.

"Thanks, Eli!" Nara said. It just didn't seem like they could fight all of these Plumbers themselves. He couldn't even be sure how many there were, or how many more would come. "You've got this, Mama?" he asked. She nodded, continuing her protective spell. Taking a deep breath, Nara removed his good hand from the woman's shoulder and turned back to Gran, laying serenely in the hospital bed. He didn't know anything about the numbers on the monitors, but the gradually lowering peaks of what he took to be her heartbeat didn't give him much hope. He placed the gota between their hands again, closing his eyes and praying wordlessly for her to return to them.

Light fell upon Nara's closed eyes, prompting him to open them. Gran had begun to glow, or more specifically, her bones glowed, showing through her flesh and the bed clothes, her hospital gown. A shifting, pulsating, glow vacillated between the blue of the ocean in the afterworld and the green of spring leaves. Over them, something else squirmed and twisted. No, not something, many somethings, a slither of serpents resolved as his attention was subsumed by the dozens of elongated shapes wrapped around the old woman's skeleton. One became aware of his staring and turned its gaze on him.

Nara tried to step back, to release Gran's hand, but the fingers wouldn't let him go. He looked down and saw some of the snakes there tied into a Gordian knot engulfing his hand and hers. From her shoulder, another serpent tilted its head at him, then another from her knee, on and on until he had their collective attention.

"Narayan." The merest whisper of a hiss met Nara's ears, though Gran's eyes remained closed, her face passive. The sounds of the battle, of ringing blades and sizzling projectiles, faded around him as his attention was fully taken hold of.

"Are you..." he began, thinking of Carmen, what he had looked like after the black cloud had knocked away his illusion spell, "Gran?"

"We are a part of her. Every person is really a collective, myriad ideas, but also beings, a human is more of a hotel than a solitary stone." The sibilant hiss shifted tone and timbre every few words, as if each snake was contributing to the message in turn. "The gota lets you see past the illusions of this world as it helps you to form your own in the next."

"Can you help us defeat the Plumbers?"

"We have struggled against them for many centuries. Perhaps it is time to rest."

"You can't give up now. Didn't you have a purpose? The good fight against the status quo? The part of you I met in the afterworld said there's no reason to die, no need for it. You called it a scam." The snakes laughed at this, a strange pulsing series of hisses more unsettling than conveying humor.

"That does sound like me... All right, help an old woman up," Gran said. Nara renewed his grip, rather than trying to pull away, and leaned back. Aizah Leon sat up, eyes still closed, head tilted to one side.

"Come on, Gran!" Nara said. Isa looked over her shoulder.

"You got her back?" The woman asked, more than a little surprise in her voice. This quickly shifted. "Hey, Aizah..." Isa began, tone full of contrition before a Plumber swooped in, piercing the shield and nearly taking her arm off. She spat an angry word or two at the creature, swinging her own one-handed sickles, severing the creature's mantid-like limb. The weapon shimmered in red and orange as it fell, striking the linoleum floor. The point sank in a few inches. The spray of warm light from the broken end drew lines back to the Plumber's sleeve and the creature retreated, howling. The glow stretched, narrowing, then snapped, drawing back in both directions. "That'll teach you!" She roared at its back.

"No!" Eli cried out at the same time, falling back under the piercing limb of another Plumber, shoving the bed back across the smooth tiles with a little screech. Gran wavered. Nara was forced back a step, but the bed bumped Isa, knocking her forward, her face now inches from the gleaming defense.

The blue field wavered. A ring of knife-like sickle points appeared at head height, pressing into the circle as one. Nara remembered the tornado at the mountaintop again. He couldn't fly away this time, nor rise up to the next world... Was there a next world up from here? Everything he'd heard pointed to yes... But he couldn't consider that now. The world he occupied moved slow, like a nightmare.

Sickles advanced in concert, slicing toward the four of them. The atmospheric bubble around them popped, receding in a flash of irregular, intensified, glow as the energies pulled together and evaporated. Then the Plumbers were on them, skewering Isa up and down, piercing her heart from two directions. Eli was impaled by one Plumber, a sickle to each lung, while another slashed at his legs. His arms flailed up over his head toward Nara. He tried to grab one with his free hand, but he couldn't reach, the cast restricting movement as it was meant to. He dropped the laser gun, never fired, and it clattered across the floor out of sight. In a second, the larger man slipped off the bed and was hidden by it as well.

Another Plumber -were they truly endless in number?- stabbed Nara in the back, the sickle forcing him forward until it also ran through Gran's chest, impaling at least one serpent there. In the existential battle between life and death, which Gran had fought for who knew how long, this was how they all lost.

Nara felt himself slipping away, falling to pieces that would become raindrops in the next world. The drawings he had sketched when he was younger, convinced he would be an artist, a dream to which he secretly held, to the trip to the museum Carmen had reminded him of, boat rides on the harbor, walking home through the streets of the city, the smell of pizza, the eyes of the first girl he had a crush on. These things were all him, draining out, no longer his.

Nara jerked like when a cabbie stomped the breaks to avoid unmindful pedestrians. Or perhaps it was more like when one fell asleep while sitting through a long mathematics class, head bobbing back up suddenly.

Not today. The words came to him, sibilant, almost angry. His eyes fluttered open. Gran's skeleton lay in the bed, patterned and decorated with flowers and loops and hearts and laces like Dia De Los Muertos make up. The snakes were all gone. No, there was movement over the edge of the bed. Here, squirming inside his shirt. There. He turned. More slithered over Mama's shoulder. One slid into a gaping wound which closed, narrowing around the tail as it tapered and vanished into her body.

Gran? he asked silently. The Plumbers were gone, having accomplished their mission. The room stood calm, quiet, and beige again. The corusca lay, like a flat bowl with burned edges, leaning against Gran's pillow, smoking faintly.

I am here. The Plumbers did not succeed, not really. I couldn't let them. You were right. This fight is not over. I couldn't let them take you. Any of you. As he heard these words in his head, he saw Mama roll over and push herself up. A deep brown hand splayed itself on the far edge of the bed, followed after a moment by its mate, and then Eli's face, chest, and waist. Nara could see the serpents embedded in his body.

I tried so hard to save you. We all did.

Yo se, Narito. I know. And you did. Part of me will be with all of you forever. It's not what I set out for all those centuries ago, but better to pass on my experiences to you three than to feed the machine that grinds us all down. Nara felt Gran's grip loosen. Her body fell back against the bed. The monitors screamed a single high note, unwavering.

"No!" Nara cried out, squeezing the bony hand harder. But it was cold now, like paper and rocks left out in winter. He tried to step closer, tears filling his eyes, but the bed blocked him. Mama wrapped her arms around him. She leaned her head against the back of his neck.

"It's going to be OK," she whispered.

"No, it's not, she's all I had. I don't know you. I don't know anyone anymore. Nothing is like it was last week."

"No, it's not," Eli agreed, "but it never is. Time's like that."

You still have family, Narito. The hissing voice was hard to hear over his own pounding heart, his pain. *Trust them, lean on them, rebuild the family. Learn from Eli, from Isa, the others. They have much of value to teach you.*

"I will," Nara, Mama, and Eli all said at once, then looking at each other, seeing the parts of Aizah that remained with each, nodded, knowing.

"We should... probably go. The hospital workers are going to have a lot of questions, and the answers I know will only lead to more questions, then straitjackets," Nara said.

"You're not wrong, mijo," Mama said.

"Home?" Eli asked. "I'm sure they need help with the coffee shop, then we can have a nice long discussion about how this is going to work now."

"We've got a hell of a fight ahead of us," Mama said.

"For Gran," Nara said, sticking a hand out between the three of them.

"For Gran," Eli and Mama agreed, putting their hands in. The lights flickered overhead, finally coming fully back on, stirring them to action. They gathered up the magical detritus and slipped out of the hospital.

"Mama?" Nara asked as they tried to walk casually along the sidewalk toward the coffee shop, Nara in the stolen wheelchair.

"Yes, Narito?"

"Last night, did you come to the hospital disguised as Carmen?"

"No... I was busy sneaking past the guards on the building to get you the gota. Why do you ask?"

"Just thinking. He didn't remember coming to see us. He cast some kind of magic over Gran. And now he's gone... I wish I could see him once more, thank him for being there all those years and saving me one last time."

"Maybe you can," Eli said, "you never know, with the gota, or maybe he even survived but ended up in Egypt, or the rain forest. With a floodgate set up, he could have been thrown anywhere, even another plane."

"I hope you're right. I should go back and check on Rodolpho... tomorrow, though, or Tuesday. I might need a few days of straight sleep. This whole magic thing is going to take getting used to." Nara shrugged.

"You don't know the half of it," Eli agreed, "Not half of the half."

END

Special Thanks

As always, I am deeply appreciative of all those who support this writing journey on which I find myself. Prominent amongst these are my Patreon supporters, many of whom give me feedback on early drafts of the series I share with them. While this book isn't amongst those, and will be brand new to them (surprise!), their constant support has helped me overcome the roadblocks to getting more books out into the world. My main Patrons, if you will, are Cynthia, Ethan, and Marilyn, who have been with me from the start of my Patreon, and good friends before that May seven years ago when I decided I was going to start a Patreon, putting chapters out every week without a solid outline. Since then, there are others, also friends and family from various parts of my life: Byron, Grady, and Kristin.

Of course, there are also my team at Ascendent, founder w.p. Quigley and fellow writer Dan, both of whom make long days at fairs and author events more enjoyable.

I would also like to thank Stephen Black of Black Thoughts Editorial Services, without whom there would be appreciably more comma errors, general grammar SNAFUs, and a few plot holes. Any remaining typos and errors, are of course, my gift to you, the reader, to allow you to point and laugh at the silly man who thinks he can write books.

www.ingramcontent.com/pod-product-compliance
Lightning Source LLC
Chambersburg PA
CBHW070425310726
48977CB00003B/835